"I'm not afraid of you!"

Cally spoke fiercely, but her stance belied her words.

"Yes, you are," said Mike softly. "But more than that, you're afraid of yourself."

Now he really was ridiculous. What did she have to fear from herself?

Something altered in his face, and his voice was husky when he spoke. "You're afraid of this." He leaned closer until she could feel his warm breath on her lips. He paused fractionally, and she held her breath. His lips brushed hers, delicately at first, teasing and tempting them to open. After a few more feathery passes from his own firm mouth, her lips relaxed of their own volition, trembling as his assault became more demanding.

"Don't," she whispered breathlessly, but her swimming senses couldn't invest the word with any force...

Dear Reader:

Romance readers today have more choice among books than ever before. But with so many titles to choose from, deciding what to select becomes increasingly difficult.

At SECOND CHANCE AT LOVE we try to make that decision easy for you — by publishing romances of the highest quality every month. You can confidently buy any SECOND CHANCE AT LOVE romance and know it will provide you with solid romantic entertainment.

Sometimes you buy romances by authors whose work you've previously read and enjoyed — which makes a lot of sense. You're being sensible . . . and careful . . . to look for satisfaction where you've found it before.

But if you're *too* careful, you risk overlooking exceptional romances by writers whose names you don't immediately recognize. These first-time authors may be the stars of tomorrow, and you won't want to miss any of their books! At SECOND CHANCE AT LOVE, many writers who were once "new" are now the most popular contributors to the line. So trying a new writer at SECOND CHANCE AT LOVE isn't really a risk at all. Every book we publish must meet our rigorous standards — whether it's by a popular "regular" or a newcomer.

In the months to come, we urge you to watch for these names — Linda Raye, Karen Keast, Betsy Osborne, Dana Daniels, and Cinda Richards. All are dazzling new writers, an elite few whose books are destined to become "keepers." We think you'll be delighted and excited by their first books with us!

Look, too, for romances by writers with whom you're already warmly familiar: Jeanne Grant, Ann Cristy, Linda Barlow, Elissa Curry, Jan Mathews, and Liz Grady, among many others.

Best wishes,

Ellen Edwards

Ellen Edwards, Senior Editor
SECOND CHANCE AT LOVE
The Berkley Publishing Group
200 Madison Avenue
New York, N.Y. 10016

Second Chance at Love

WILDCATTER'S KISS

KELLY ADAMS

**SECOND CHANCE AT LOVE
BOOK**

Other Second Chance at Love books by
Kelly Adams

BITTERSWEET REVENGE #47
RESTLESS TIDES #113

First edition published October 1984

First printing

"Second Chance at Love" and the butterfly emblem are trademarks belonging to Jove Publications, Inc.

Printed in the United States of America

Second Chance at Love books are published by
The Berkley Publishing Group
200 Madison Avenue, New York, NY 10016

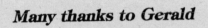

Many thanks to Gerald

splattered with the same mud, now drying to a light brown, and her red-checked flannel shirt sported a hole over the left elbow, plus the space where a missing button revealed the pink bow adorning the front of her bra whenever she spread her arms. She probably looked like a wild woman, she thought in exasperation. Her wide gray eyes and black hair gave her an exotic look that turned heads wherever she went. Boy, could she turn some heads today!

The previous week she'd maneuvered the old churn drill, a vintage Bucyrus Erie that once belonged to her grandfather, to her drilling site about a quarter mile from the farmhouse, at the edge of her soybean field. Setting the jacks to level the drill and cleaning up the equipment had gobbled up the rest of her time. She crawled into bed half-asleep every night and didn't even remember pulling up the covers. That every muscle was as tight as the sausage casings in Leffert's Meat Shop was testimony to the work she'd done.

Well, the rig was cleaned up now, and she ran a critical eye over it. Her grandfather had drilled water wells until the day he died, at the age of ninety-three, and no one had touched the rig since. "There's oil in these rocks," he'd told Cally more than once, and she'd often gone to sleep dreaming of hitting a gusher.

Time had proved him right. This section of western Illinois had oil deposits, though they weren't huge. What made drilling lucrative was the fact that the deposits were located only seven hundred feet below the surface.

Cally climbed onto the truck bed and started the engine, then pulled the gear to raise the derrick. Groaning and protesting, the derrick gradually assumed an upright position, forty feet straight up, and Cally dusted her hands in satisfaction. The cable still looked good. The next step was to retie the stinger, the six-inch-long piece of metal that housed the cable and in turn slipped into the metal drill tool. She played out the cable until the stinger touched the ground, then squatted down and went to work on it. There was an opening in one side through which the end of the cable had to be pulled. Cally yelped as the fingernail on her right index finger bent back. Jerking her hand to her mouth, she sucked on the sore finger delicately until it stopped throbbing, then inspected it. No doubt the nail would break by

Chapter One

CALLY TAYLOR HAD dragged her aching body out of bed at sunup—literally dragged—and in her opinion nothing much had improved in the ensuing four hours. She rocked back on her heels and glared at the faded-green churn drill, the source of her bad mood. With its drilling derrick folded neatly above the truck bed it looked like a pickup truck pumping iron. But despite her backbreaking efforts of the past week, the drill still wasn't operational.

White fleecy clouds scuttled overhead in an endless blue sky, and a spring breeze ruffled the heads of the daffodils she'd so lovingly planted by the driveway four years ago. But even an early May day in Prairie Junction, Illinois, so welcome because it came on the heels of a particularly blustery winter, couldn't cheer her up.

"That's right," she muttered in the general direction of the daffodils. "Say 'I told you so.'" The daffodils nodded their heads in unison, like a cluster of bonnet-clad gossips.

She brushed back her long black hair, which had escaped the confines of two neat barrettes exactly three hours ago, then groaned when she glanced down and saw the mud on her hands. Well, it didn't matter anyway. Her hair would need a thorough washing by tonight. In fact, the smartest thing would be to walk through a car wash. Her jeans were

1

WILDCATTER'S KISS

the end of the day. At least all her fingers were starting to look uniform, she thought in resignation. It would probably be a good six months before her nails were long enough to wear polish again.

She'd just worked the cable through the hole when the fingernail broke, and Cally applied first aid in the form of her mouth again. She was sucking on her finger, ruminating on the sad state of the farm, when she heard the first low rumblings of an approaching truck. Glaring over her shoulder, she watched the bright red Donovan Drilling truck make its way over the edge of her field on the west side of her property. George Fanning had hired the drilling company three days ago, and for three days they'd driven across her field without so much as a by-your-leave or thank you. The winter wheat in that field was coming up in bright green stalks, and she shuddered to think of the damage wreaked by the truck. Fanning had waged a running feud with Cally's late husband Dan about the property line, and it seemed he claimed another inch every year.

She looked down at the cable cutter, a mini-guillotine, malevolent thoughts forming, then sighed and stood up. She could be civil about this, she told herself. She really could. She wouldn't let what happened to her and Dan affect the way she dealt with the Donovan Drilling Company. She'd be polite even though wildcatters—independent drillers—weren't her favorite slice of humanity.

By the time Cally had walked to the house, where her pickup was parked, the Donovan truck had made another trip through her wheat field, and her temperature was rising fast. Her yellow pickup hadn't run well when Dan was alive, and it hadn't improved any since his death. It moaned and wheezed for a full minute, then reluctantly chugged to life. Cally slammed the clutch to the floor and ground the gearshift into first. She drove toward the back of the house, where the gravel drive became more of a path, then turned right to follow the fence bordering the feedlot. Fresh-faced heifers bawled at her as the truck passed, then backed away, wide-eyed. The path followed the northern edge of the wheat field, at a right angle to the path the Donovan truck had taken. As Cally approached the end of the field she saw the bright red pickup returning, and she ground her teeth. The truck beat her to the intersection of their paths, and she saw a flash of white teeth as the driver smiled and waved. Muttering under her breath, Cally glanced furiously at the flattened rows of winter wheat, now brown and muddy, before she spun out after the truck. Her bald tires slipped on the slick dirt, then recovered. Damn, she needed a new truck. But she also needed the money to buy one. And the prices of corn and wheat were down this year, while those of seed and fertilizer were up.

There would be enough money if it hadn't been for the drilling company that had fleeced Dan the year before he died. They'd assured him they'd find oil; then they'd talked him into sinking all his savings—even borrowing on his life insurance policy—into drilling expenses. They never found oil, but then they never looked very hard either. They were there about four days, then left town as quickly as they'd come, like a bad storm. Lots of other farmers had been taken in, too, and when Dan and the others finally investigated, they discovered that the company wasn't legitimate. Dan was never the same after that, and she had a sad suspicion that the day the tractor turned over on him on a steep grade, he had been careless because his mind was on the savings he'd lost.

The faster Donovan truck had outdistanced Cally, but she caught sight of a red derrick ahead. The gate between her fence line and George Fanning's was ajar, and Cally accelerated. The truck backfired, and Cally patted its dashboard soothingly. "Come on, Daffy," she murmured encouragingly. The truck had been bright yellow when Dan bought it, used, so they'd begun calling it Daffodil. That was the same fall Cally planted the row of daffodils down the drive.

She topped a small hill and jammed on the brakes when she saw the Donovan truck stopped straight ahead in her path. Daffy squealed in protest, and the bald tires skidded like a sled on ice. Cally felt the rear end going sideways, and she murmured a quick prayer for the red truck to just disappear, but miraculously Daffy came to a mud-splattering halt at a right angle to the other truck, only inches from its fender. Gingerly, Cally let her muscles relax and looked around. Three men in dirty jeans and cotton shirts rolled up to the elbows stood staring at her, reminding her of the heifers that congregated at the fence to watch her passing in pop-eyed fascination.

She took a deep breath and studied the three before trusting her legs to carry her from the truck. The first was a young boy, probably just out of high school, tall and lean, a pack of cigarettes in his rolled-up sleeve. Tough kid who thinks he owns the world, she mentally categorized him. The second was much older, in his sixties by the look of the grizzled white stubble on his chin and the large bald spot he was now scratching as he stared back at her. Probably a real grump. These two were definitely the hired workers—roughnecks.

She turned her attention to the third man and found a pair of steely blue eyes staring back with cool appraisal. In an instant she knew this man was the boss—the "tool pusher" in driller's jargon. He was in his thirties, deeply tanned from outdoor work, sun-bleached streaks in wavy, dark brown hair. He stood with hands on hips as though expecting a confrontation. Well, he wasn't going to be disappointed.

Cally took her time climbing down, concentrating on presenting a composed exterior. But she found her heart racing every time she glanced at the third man, the boss. He was taller than the other two, over six feet, she guessed. When it came time to pass out rugged handsomeness, this man must have gotten in line twice. Everything about him said charisma, from the tan, aristocratic face, to his stance, straight and uncompromising. His lips parted slightly when she stepped from behind the truck, and she stared at them as if she'd never seen lips before. At least she hadn't seen any with the sensual promise of these. Firm and full, they seemed to beckon to her. Her hypnotic trance abruptly broke when she turned her ankle in a deep rut in the road. Her eyes were still on him, and he stepped forward with lightning speed the instant she stumbled, but she caught herself, her breath suspended as he stopped only a foot away from her.

"Are you all right?" he asked in a low, husky voice. "That was quite an entrance in your truck."

His voice enveloped her like a gentle embrace, and Cally shivered despite the spring sun. She was beginning to guess at the seductive prowess of the man, if the force of his presence was any indication. A warning bell rang in her head. Air raid. Dangerous man. You might get involved. Instinctively she drew back, physically and emotionally. "I didn't know you'd be parked in the middle of the road," she said.

The man looked at her curiously, seeming to measure her before he spoke again. "Are you related to George Fanning?"

Cally snorted in derision. "The only thing he and I have in common is a fence line that he keeps pushing farther onto my property."

"So you're Cally Taylor," he said with a slow smile that made her uneasy. "Mr. Fanning told us about you."

"And despite what he told you, I don't steal his pumpkins or cut down his walnut trees, even though he's accused me of both."

"And you're not a dried-up old crone with flint where your heart should be." This time she was sure there was laughter behind his words.

Cally gasped in fury. "He told you that? Why, that old buzzard! If he weren't seventy-five years old I'd bounce one of his damn pumpkins off his hard head."

The blue eyes were crinkling, and a mischievous smile played about those lips. "Now hold on. George didn't exactly say all those things. I just inferred them from his tone. Sounds like the two of you don't get along very well."

"That's an understatement," she said dryly. "Two years ago someone stole some of his pumpkins, and he came roaring over to my house and accused me because I had a bunch of my own sitting on the porch. I was canning pumpkin. I told him it was probably the drillers, but he—" She broke off suddenly, realizing what she'd let slip.

His eyes darkened, but there was no other discernible change in his expression. "A regular Hatfield and McCoy feud," he observed quietly.

"It's been going on for years." She took a deep breath and looked him square in the face. The damage had been done with her remark about drillers. She might as well forget tact. "I imagine he told you to drive over the field to your site, but you're ruining my winter wheat." She pointed vigorously at her smashed wheat, quickly lowering her arm when she saw his eyes fall to her open shirt.

"So that's your field. He said you wouldn't mind."

"Wouldn't mind?" Cally sputtered. "Naturally I enjoy watching you smash down part of my crop every day. I'm only farming for fun. Money means nothing." Her temper rising in the face of his implacable calm, she uttered the last with biting sarcasm.

"The creek is up over his road," the man explained, as if she'd said nothing. "The gully's too deep to drive through."

"So you'll keep driving over my wheat?" she demanded angrily. "I might have known. You're just like the last bunch that was here. Just drill and collect the money for finding nothing. Well, I'm not going to stand by and let it go this time. I'm going to call your boss—what's his name?—Donovan. And I'm going to tell him that I'm lodging a complaint with the sheriff unless you stop driving over my field." She glanced at the pickup truck and saw ST. LOUIS in smaller letters under the name. "And maybe when he hears about this he'll come up here and do something." She finished her tirade and glared at the man, her hands jammed into the pockets of her jeans.

"Are you finished?" he asked calmly.

She stared back at him in disbelief. "I don't think we have anything to discuss," she said, and turned to leave.

A strong hand on her arm halted her departure. She turned back angrily, dimly aware of a growing warmth spreading up her arm, touching nerves that had lain as dormant as seeds under frozen earth. "Let go of me," she said, her voice shaking.

His hand gradually loosened its hold and lowered to his side, but his piercing eyes held her motionless. "I'm Mike Donovan," he said quietly. "Your business is with me."

Cally stood transfixed, her arm still burning from his touch. The light breeze suddenly picked up and ruffled her hair, bringing her out of her trance. She raked her hair back with one hand. Her agitation must have showed, because he relaxed his shoulders and gave her a humorless smile. "We won't drive over your fields anymore, Mrs. Taylor, if you'll allow us to use your drive to reach the gate."

She gathered her wits and then her voice, which seemed to be lost somewhere in her shoes. "Yes, of course. That would be fine."

"Good." There was warmth in his smile now, and Cally felt as though she were walking to a warm fire after being out in the cold a long time. "These are my friends and fellow workers." Cally blinked and looked over at the other two men. Mike Donovan's presence was so absorbing that she'd forgotten there was anyone else there. "This is Tom Peterson." The young boy smiled hesitantly. "And this is Happy Jack. His given name, which I don't think even his daughter remembers now, is Harold Jackson."

The bald man smiled a toothy grin and ran his thumbs under the top of his overalls. "Pleased to meet you, Mrs. Taylor."

"That looked like an old Bucyrus Erie you have," Donovan said. "Is it yours?"

Cally nodded. "It was my grandfather's."

"You're doing some drilling?" he persisted.

"Working on it," Cally said hesitantly. Standing beside Mike Donovan's shiny red hydraulic rig, she realized how ancient her churn drill must appear. Like a dinosaur on a city street.

"By yourself?" He sounded incredulous now, and Cally stiffened.

"I'd better get going," she said, backing away. "Thank you for not driving over my field."

She knew they were watching her as she climbed back into her truck, and she cursed under her breath when Daffy wouldn't start. Just like a truck to conk out when you needed it most. Just as she saw Donovan move from the corner of her eye, the engine coughed to life, and the cab shook with the motor's spasms. Cally gave the men a curt nod and pulled away. When she reached her house she sat in the truck a few minutes, rubbing her arm. She could still feel the heated imprint of each finger, though he hadn't held her tightly. She was afraid that if she pushed up her shirt sleeve she'd see a permanent imprint of his hand, like a mark of ownership.

She bristled again at the memory of his calm, self-assured manner. He was better looking than the other drillers who'd come, and smoother, but that was all surface. Underneath he was just like they were—out for whatever he could get.

She might as well drive on down to the rig and try to finish tying the stinger, she decided. It wasn't lunchtime yet. The daffodils nodded at her passing, and she remembered how Dan had told her the bulbs were too expensive. "We could sure use the money for something useful," he'd said. "Don't be so extravagant, honey." She cried herself to sleep that night, hating the fact that there wasn't enough money for pretty things like flowers. For her birthday her mother had sent her a large package of daffodil bulbs. Dan just shook his head.

She hadn't thought of that in years. She hadn't thought of a lot of things. There was no time or energy for memories. After Dan died, it was sheer force of will that kept her going, feeding and watering the livestock, cutting the grass, weeding the vegetable garden. Friends advised her to sell the farm—it was too much work, they said—but she couldn't sell it, not yet. It was Dan's farm, and she felt she owed it to him to keep it going. Her heart wouldn't let go yet.

She stopped beside the churn drill and rubbed her eyes wearily. Work made her forget about Dan and the accident and the pressures of the farm. Work was all she'd known for a year now. No. Also for the four years she and Dan had been married before his death. He'd just purchased the farm when they met, and he was full of grandiose plans. They'd build a herd of champion Herefords together, he told her. They'd renovate the old farmhouse into a showcase. And they'd get one of those drillers passing through to drill a couple of oil wells on their land. Then they'd be rich.

Cally stepped out of the truck and looked around dispiritedly. Plans were all they ever had. The old house was still as cold as creek water in mid-January every time the wind howled and rattled the shutters. The only redecorating they'd managed to accomplish was to hang some second-hand venetian blinds. Plaster flaked off the walls, and there were large cracks above the doorframes. The walls and siding badly needed a new coat of paint. "Like a poor old lady," Cally muttered to the house. "You're stooped and faded and can't afford a new winter coat." The signs of neglect were everywhere she looked, so Cally resolutely stopped looking. There was only so much she could do.

The stinger cable severed when she struck the cutting tool with a sledgehammer, and she struggled to pull the cut ends out and up, tying them to the cable. That accomplished, she poked the cable back into the stinger, sighing wearily. She put on a heavy leather glove and built a small fire in a portable cookstove, then held the metal ladle filled with babbitt over it. The babbitt, a mixture of tin, copper, and antimony, would seal the ends tightly so the stinger wouldn't slip off the cable.

When she finally finished and glanced at her watch it was noon. Rocking back on her heels, she surveyed her work. Not bad. It was a good thing she'd watched her grandfather when she was little. She'd remembered how he'd done it. She stood up gingerly, her knees stiff, and stretched. Her stomach rumbled, and she mentally evaluated the contents of her refrigerator. She'd finished off the last piece of apple pie for breakfast. That left her a choice of two tablespoons of cottage cheese a week past the expiration date on the carton, half a bottle of root beer, the fruitcake her Aunt Frieda sent last Christmas, or something green and fuzzy in the vegetable bin. She should have gone to the grocery store yesterday, but she'd been so busy setting up the drilling rig that she hadn't had time. The next best thing to her refrigerator was the diner half a mile down the road. She had a suspicion they had green, fuzzy things in their vegetable bins, too, but she hadn't died from the hamburgers yet.

She checked her pockets for the five-dollar bill she'd stuck there this morning, then climbed into the truck and started it up. "Well, what do you know," she murmured in satisfaction when the engine purred at the first turn of the ignition key. "Maybe things are going to go right for a change."

She pulled out onto the blacktop, splashing through a deep, rain-filled rut at the end of her drive. Cally twisted the radio dial, thumping the steering wheel in time to Michael Jackson's "Beat It." This was a college radio station with squeaky-voiced announcers. The two other area radio stations played polka music interspersed with liberal doses of farm market reports.

There was a new thump out of beat with the music, and it suddenly dawned on her that it came from the truck. It was a chug followed by a wheeze, then another chug. Cally maneuvered the truck to the side of the road just as the last chug died into silence. "Come on, Daffy," she pleaded, pumping the gas pedal as she turned the ignition key. There was a moment of hope as the engine coughed once, but it was apparently a last gasp; there was no more life to be wrung from it. "Damn," she muttered, leaning back in the seat and closing her eyes.

She sat that way another couple of minutes, fervently hoping the engine would revive itself like Lazarus if she just gave it time. Her eyes were still shut when she heard a truck slow down on the blacktop and come to a halt.

"Having trouble?"

Her eyes flew open and she choked back a dismayed expletive. Stopped next to her was the Donovan Drilling truck, and the young boy, Tom, was smiling at her.

"It'll be okay in a minute," she assured him, seeing Happy in the middle and Mike behind the wheel. Mike was leaning one arm against the dashboard, looking across at her. Quickly she turned the key again, desperately praying the engine would start. But it coughed again and lapsed into deathly silence.

She heard Mike say something to the others, and then he was getting out of the truck. He lifted her hood without even asking—talk about nerve!—and began fiddling with something she couldn't identify. "Get me that can out of the back," he called to Tom, and the boy hopped out to do his bidding. Cally was fuming in the cab as Tom handed Mike the can and Mike sprayed under the hood. Standing back, he wiped his hands on his jeans and said, "Okay, try her now."

Skeptical, Cally turned the key, startled when the engine leaped to life. She gave a couple of exploratory pushes on the gas pedal, but the truck rocked with exuberance instead of dying. "That should do it," Mike said, slamming the hood and coming around to the side. "You got the distributor cap wet when you ran through some water." He turned to Tom. "I think I'll ride with her and make sure she makes it okay." They pulled away, and he came around to the passenger side, sliding in beside her.

"You know, you didn't even ask where I'm going," she said peevishly, checking the rearview mirror before she pulled back onto the road.

He gave her a lazy grin that reminded her all over again of the touch of his hand. "Since it's noon, I figured you were headed somewhere with food, which is where I'm going. But I'll ask anyway. Where are you going?"

"Gordon's Grill," she said in resignation. "Is that where you were headed?"

He leaned back and stretched, his hands behind his head. "It's the only place to eat we could find around here. Isn't there anything else?"

"Well, there's the Dairy Freeze. They microwave frozen hamburgers."

"No thanks," he said dryly. "I guess it's Gordon's Grill."

He lapsed into silence, and she stole a glance at him. He was staring straight ahead, seemingly lost in thought, his eyes half-closed. He looked tired, she thought, surprised that such an observation could touch her. There was that chink in her armor again, feeling something for a man she disliked.

"You've done a lot of work on that old Bucyrus Erie," he observed quietly, startling her. "Looked like you were tying a new stinger today."

"Um-hmmm."

There was another silence, then he said, "Drillers don't take an oath of silence about their work, you know. I'm not going to race right over and move my drill to your site."

Cally sighed. "I'm sorry, Mr. Donovan. There's nothing to talk about. We're almost at the diner anyway."

"What about less formality, Cally?" When she didn't say anything he said, "Come on. Just say 'Mike.'"

"What?"

"Just say it."

She shrugged. "Mike."

"Very good. Now we're on a first-name basis. And that entitles us to have a conversation. I get to ask a reasonable question, and you get to give a civil answer. All right?"

"I'm sorry, Mr. Donovan. I don't mean to be rude, but I'm not in a talkative mood."

"I can see you're still having trouble grasping this concept," he said with a solemn shake of his head. "Now, repeat after me. Mike."

"Mike—" she began in exasperation, but he cut her off.

"Good. Now say 'Mike, would you have lunch with me?'"

A smile tugged at her mouth in spite of her determination.

"Hey, I think you're getting in the spirit of this thing," he said.

Cally turned the truck into the diner parking lot, noting the Donovan truck was already there. Mike hopped out and reached up to help her down when she opened her door. Again, the touch of his hand on her arm sent pleasurable shivers telegraphing messages to every nerve ending. "Come on," he said, taking her hand. "I'll slip the maître d' a tenspot and we'll get the best table in the house."

Gordon, the diner's pudgy cook and owner, acknowledged their entrance with a salute of his spatula; then he turned back to the grill behind the counter, wiping one greasy hand on an apron that might possibly have been white at one time.

Tom and Happy were sitting in a booth near the door, sipping coffee. "Looks like you got it fixed all right," Tom observed, grinning at them. "Mike can fix anything. Anything," he repeated with a knowing smile that implied that Mike had already fixed whatever was wrong with Cally.

"Obviously he's very talented with machinery," Cally agreed smoothly, emphasizing the last word. She moved on down the diner to slide into a booth at the back, nodding to local farmers she knew. She glanced up in surprise when Mike slid in opposite her. "Aren't you eating with your friends?"

"I can eat with them anytime. And you did ask me to lunch, didn't you?" His smile was beguiling, and Cally found herself softening.

"Not in so many words," she said.

"Then repeat after me. Mike, join me for lunch."

She found herself smiling back. "Mike, join me for lunch,"

she said with a shake of her head and a remonstrative glance at him.

"There, that wasn't so bad, was it? Now I'll press my luck and ask again about the Bucyrus Erie. I used to have one myself, you know."

"You?"

"Don't sound so surprised. It was all I could afford when I first started out."

"Oh. I just assumed you inherited the business. I mean you're so . . . uh, established in business."

"If you were about to say I'm young, I'll take that as a compliment," he said, his eyes sparkling. "I worked hard to build up the business. Now, what are you doing with your grandfather's old churn drill?"

"I'm going to drill for oil," Cally said defensively, watching for his reaction.

He took a deep breath before answering. "That's tough work."

"For a woman," she amended coolly.

"For anyone. Especially alone. And especially with a churn drill."

She was about to defend herself, but the waitress, Reba, dropped two menus on the table. "Hi, Cally," she said, snapping her gum. "How ya doin', Mike?"

Cally looked at him quickly and saw him grin at the girl. "Just fine, Reba. How's my favorite waitress?"

From the smile Reba gave him, Cally knew that the girl's pleasantness was more than just a ploy for a big tip. Apparently Mike Donovan had already gotten to work on the local women.

"Special today's meatloaf," Reba said. "And we've got some of that chocolate pie you like, Mike."

"Sounds good. How about you, Cally? Meatloaf and chocolate pie all right?"

"I'll take the diet platter," she said crisply.

Mike shook his head. "Bring her the meatloaf."

When Reba had slithered away, her hips preceding the rest of her body like a majorette leading a marching band, Cally turned on him irritably. "Do you always force your preferences on other people?"

"Um-hmmm," he commented, refusing to argue with

her. "I'm an absolute dictator. Now tell me about your drill rig."

It was useless to argue with him; she could see that. "All right. I'll tell you about the rig."

"That's better." She bristled at his satisfied tone, but when she glared at him she saw he was smiling.

"My grandfather drilled water wells. I used to go with him when I was little. I loved to fall asleep at night in my sleeping bag listening to that steady *chunk, chunk* of the drill. It was like a lullaby. He had endless patience. He'd answer all my questions and show me how to do everything he did. I was too small to handle the heavy work, but I loved pretending."

"You got the drill after he died?"

"Sort of. It was just sitting around at my parents' house, so I cleaned it up and brought it to the farm after my husband died." Afraid he might ask questions about Dan, she hurried on, twisting her paper napkin in her fingers. "I've got it just about ready to go now."

"What got you interested in drilling for oil?"

"My husband always wanted to find oil on our property. Unfortunately, things didn't work out." She said the last with more than a touch of acrimony, thinking about the drillers who'd cheated them. "So I got together with John Masters, my neighbor on the east side, and he's covering the costs of fixing up the rig, getting casing, license fees, all that. I'll drill one hole on my property, then one on his and so on."

"That could take a long time." He leaned back as Reba set two Cokes in front of them, pushing her cleavage forward as she bent over close to Mike. *Special today, melons,* Cally thought dryly. Reba put some extra oomph into her rear as she sauntered away, and when Cally looked at Mike she found him grinning at her. "Quite a menu she has," he observed.

"All available for the asking," Cally retorted.

"I don't like women who hang everything out for the taking," he said, his eyes never leaving her face.

"Oh." She lowered her eyes and busied herself fingering the red tape covering the rip in the booth's seat. She could feel the pulse pounding in her throat, so hard it must be visible. Self-consciously she held her hand to her neck, pretending to massage it.

She was rescued from Mike's scrutiny when Reba returned a moment later with two plates of meatloaf, mashed potatoes and gravy, bread and corn. Cally had to admit she was glad Mike had cancelled her diet plate. She was ravenous.

She came up for air several minutes later, her plate cleaned, and saw him watching her. Embarrassed, she wiped her mouth and took a swallow of Coke. "I guess I was pretty hungry."

"I'd hate to see what you'd have done to the diet plate," he commented, and Cally opened her mouth to angrily defend herself before she realized he was teasing her.

Reba brought two pieces of chocolate pie drowning in whipped cream, and Cally ignored Mike's amused glance as she dug in. Reba's gum-snapping increased in tempo, and Cally glanced up to see the redhead smiling at Mike. "Sure you don't want anything else?" she asked him seductively.

"Just the check," he said smoothly.

She shrugged and turned the check facedown on the table, giving Cally an over-the-shoulder look as she walked away that said Cally was a waste of Mike's time.

They finished their pie in silence. Cally surreptitiously studying him from under lowered lashes. He seemed so cool and collected that she wondered if he ever lost his temper.

"That was good," he said, pushing away the plate. "Now aren't you glad I ordered for you?"

"Sure you don't want anything else?" she teased, mimicking Reba.

The grin he gave her was wicked. "Lady, you definitely should not ask me that question. What else I'd like from you isn't on the menu."

Cally felt her throat go dry. His blue eyes were seductively inviting, making promises she didn't want to think about.

"Don't worry," he said with a husky laugh. "I'm not going to make any sudden moves here in the restaurant. But look out. If the opportunity presents itself . . ."

He didn't need to complete the sentence. Cally understood all too well what he meant. She'd heard his line before—from other drillers. She knew exactly what Mike Donovan wanted. "Your friends are done," she said with icy reserve. "You'd better hurry."

He glanced back at them. "I think I'll ride back with you to make sure the truck keeps running."

"That won't be necessary," she said quickly, reaching for the check. His hand closed on hers, stopping her heart. "Cally," he said in a low voice, like a cat mesmerizing a mouse. "Don't be so damned independent. I could help you with the drilling."

"And what would your price be?" she asked coldly, despite the catch in her throat. She felt his hand tighten. "What you could get for free from Reba?"

"No price," he said in a voice thick with an anger that made her shiver. "I don't put price tags on people, Cally."

"Don't you?" She stared back, her eyes indicting him. "Isn't that what this lunch has been all about? Be nice to the lady, flatter her. Then see if you can get a little extra business from her, and—oh, yes—maybe sleep with her on the side. Makes you a winner all the way around, doesn't it, Mike Donovan?" If her anger hadn't inflamed her senses to white-hot she would have shuddered at the look on his face. People were beginning to turn around to look at them, and Cally jerked her hand free.

"Here," she said, throwing her five-dollar bill on the table. "Now I don't owe you anything." She backed away from the table, unable to stop looking at him. Tearing her eyes away, she hurried down the aisle toward the door, ignoring the startled looks from Tom and Happy at the register.

Everything was a blur as she got in the pickup and slammed the door. She cursed when the engine refused to start immediately. Then it turned over, and she threw it in reverse, spinning gravel as she backed out onto the road. Mike's face swam before her, and she blinked furiously.

Chapter Two

CALLY HADN'T SLEPT WELL. She told herself the weather forecast was the root of her irritability. Rain would delay everything—the corn planting and her drilling—as well as endanger the new litters of pigs. But under duress she might have admitted that her encounter with Mike Donovan had upset her.

After several predawn hours of tossing and turning, telling herself she could sleep if she just closed her eyes and relaxed, she finally got up and padded to the kitchen in her fluffy bedroom slippers and a worn Japanese kimono, which she only kept because she loved it, to make tea.

She pressed her eyes tightly closed now as she leaned against the stove, waiting for the water to boil, but it was the same as when she was in bed. She kept seeing him. Instead of counting sheep, she'd found herself daydreaming at five A.M., counting the dark hairs on his sideburns and the flecks of gold in his blue eyes. She was definitely losing her mind.

The other time a stranger had touched her, when Dan was still alive, no guilty memories had plagued her. She'd been angry—oh, had she been angry!—but once she'd vented her spleen on the hapless man she hadn't given him a second thought.

He'd been a driller, too, another bad apple in the group
that cheated Dan. She'd gone out to the drilling site in the
pickup the first day they were there to see if the man wanted
some lemonade. Crows had invaded the cornfield, scream-
ing in a frenzy as her truck sent them scattering to the sky
like an explosion of ink droplets. He was drilling alone that
day, and he was hot and sweaty. He stopped to lean against
the truck, wiping his brow. After a few sips, he'd smiled
at her with a slanted look, and his finger had touched her
bare shoulder. Too repulsed to move, she felt creeping horror when his hand began wandering down the front of her
halter top. Finding her voice somehow in the chaotic fury
consuming her, she jerked away and pushed his hand violently. She couldn't remember now what she'd said—a
more vituperative version of *Don't ever touch me again*,
she guessed. She'd roared away in the truck, letting the tires
spit gravel at his shoes.

She really hadn't thought of him much since then. She'd
never mentioned the incident to Dan, even after the drillers
abruptly left town, leaving behind promises and empty wal-
lets. But the incident had lurked in the back of her mind,
sparking a violent reaction to Mike's offer to help her with
the drilling. It was true that she wasn't married now. But
she still felt something illicit about his interest, as though
he would make demands she couldn't meet.

The shrill whistling of the teakettle brought her back to
the present, and she poured the water into the heavy-duty
ceramic pot, a dull brown. The Christmas before Dan died
she told him she'd like one of those oriental china teapots.
She especially liked one she'd seen in the pharmacy, an
eggshell color with pink roses and gold filigree leaves. But
Dan said she wasn't being practical. With farmhands in and
out of the house the pot was sure to get broken. And what
use were little cups without handles anyway? She'd brought
it up again the next time they were in the pharmacy together,
and he was even more impatient.

She dropped the chamomile-filled infuser into the pot
and fished in the cupboard for the honey. The first pale
edges of dawn were showing on the horizon over her field,
a soft pink as delicate as a drop of strawberry juice. The
wheat looked good this year. If she could show just a little

profit she could add a couple more cattle to the herd.

Cally poured the tea into a white mug with Christmas holly and berries on it. The mug had been free with the purchase of a roast beef sandwich at a hamburger chain in Quincy, the nearest town of any size. Though not overly large, Quincy had all the amenities—fast-food restaurants serving everything from fried chicken to hamburgers, and enough pizza parlors to satisfy the most discriminating teenager.

She was just opening the honey when there was a tap on the door. Startled, she nearly dropped the jar. Her first thought was that her cousin Donna had dropped by, but it took her only a split second to figure out that Donna was not about to be anywhere but in bed at five A.M. As Cally's mother was fond of pointing out, Donna had "married well"— a lawyer. She lived in a brick home in Quincy with two lovely children and a maid, and shopped in St. Louis. She dabbled in real estate. And she didn't get up at five A.M.

It was John Masters at the door, and Cally immediately asked if anything was wrong. His wife Paula had been sick with the flu, and with her arthritis her health was often tenuous.

"No, she's almost well now," John said, cap in hand as he scraped his work boots on the doormat. "I was setting out to cut some dead trees by the fence line and I saw your light."

"Come on in. I just made some tea, but I have some instant coffee here somewhere."

"Don't bother. I'll just stay a minute." He stood by the door looking pained, and Cally knew it would take several more minutes before he got around to telling her why he'd stopped by.

"Sit down a minute anyway," she offered, and he nodded. She carried her tea to the table and took the chair opposite him. John was a big man, in his fifties, tall and broad-shouldered, with a full head of graying hair. He and Paula had never had children, and they'd become Cally's second family when Dan died. They were always there whenever she needed them, and she knew she could never repay them for the kindness they assumed was second nature to the whole world.

"One of your heifers was in the bean field yesterday," John said. "I ran her back in the feedlot."

"Thanks. I'm putting them into the pasture tomorrow. I'm going to have to do some work on that fence on the east side. It's getting rotten."

"It'll hold a while longer, leastways till you put calves in the feedlot again. I patched the bad spot for you."

"Thanks, John. I appreciate it."

"No trouble." He cleared his throat. "Cally, about this drilling."

Her heart sank. Surely he wasn't going to tell her he'd changed his mind. Their agreement was that John would pay for the casing and supplies, and Cally would do the actual drilling. Without his financial support, she couldn't afford to continue drilling after the first two holes.

"I think we need some outside help," he said, splaying his calloused hands on the table. "It could take months with that churn drill, and I hate to see you work like that. I'd help you, but I don't have the time with all the farm work. And I'm not young anymore."

"John, I understand. It's all right. You can hire someone else to do the drilling." She hoped she sounded convincing, because disappointment had her near tears.

His face relaxed into a smile. "Thanks, Cally. I knew you'd understand. Now, the drillers I thought to hire have to drive forty miles to the nearest motel, which runs them into money for gas. So I suggested we put them up. Their boss thought it was a great idea. And he said he could knock quite a bit off each hole that way. He'll drill first on my place, then yours. I'll pay for each hole."

His words were twirling in Cally's head like dry leaves in a windstorm. "Put them up?" she repeated. That was the only thing that had jumped out at her right away.

"Yeah, we've only got the two bedrooms, so we thought you could house a couple of them. One of them's an older fella, so he'll be like a chaperon. I hope you don't mind, but what with Paula's health now, I don't think she can take care of four."

"You mean have two of them sleep here?" she said, her eyes fixed on John as though he might disappear into thin air any minute, taking this strange proposition with him.

She had a feeling of foreboding, and she took another sip of tea to quell it.

"You wouldn't have to cook or anything, and they'd supply their own groceries. I'm sure they wouldn't even be around all that much. Drilling is pretty much a sunup-to-sundown job, Mr. Donovan said."

"Mr. Donovan?" Cally's mouth had gone dry, and all the tea in the world couldn't moisten it.

"The boss. I talked to him yesterday. He said he can bring up another worker from St. Louis, since there's three of them now. He says they can work two rigs at once that way. I talked to him yesterday while he was drilling on old man Fanning's property. Donovan seems like a sharp young fellow to me. Says he thinks there's oil around here, enough to make a good profit. He's a good worker, not like that bunch that came through here couple of years ago." His eyes suddenly filled with contrition, and he rubbed his hand over his stubbly chin. "Sorry, Cally."

"That's all right," she said, still in a daze. "It doesn't bother me anymore."

"Well, I'll sure be glad to get you away from that damn old piece of metal you been working with. Bothered me every time I saw you down there by it."

He stood up to leave, and Cally pushed away her tea. The honey had turned bitter. "John," she said quietly, "I can't house the Donovan people."

He looked at her in surprise. "What's wrong, Cally? Like I said, it wouldn't be much work. If you're worried about what people would say, there's no need. The old man would stay here, too. You've had field hands sleep over before."

"But these are drillers, John. Not field hands." She was surprised at the steely bitterness in her voice, and she watched John's eyes cloud over.

He sighed heavily. "Well, I guess if your mind's made up, then that's that. I'll just have to tell 'em to forget it. They've got plenty of work to do anyway."

"You could go ahead and have them drill for you," she said.

John shook his head, twisting his cap in his hands. "Naw, can't put all that on Paula. Two guys staying at the house is no problem." He shook his head again. "But I can't ask

Paula to look after four. She's not up to it."

Cally realized the bind she was in. John would never ask her to do something she was opposed to, but she owed him, owed him a great deal. And she owed Paula. She wasn't sure she could have made it without them after Dan died. John would never say anything about her refusal; it would be as though it never happened. But he wouldn't understand. To him, friends and neighbors could always be relied on for help.

John was walking slowly to the door, putting on his cap. "Well, I'll see you later, Cally. Take care."

"John, I've changed my mind. Tell the men they can stay here." She said it quickly, before she could change her mind again, then clenched her teeth to hold back a grimace.

"Thanks, Cally." He broke into a grin. "Whew, I'm glad you said that. I'm really excited about this drilling. And it's got Paula going, too. I'll tell Mr. Donovan. So long." He fairly ran out the door, a new spring in his step. How easy it was to say the words that made him so happy, and how hard to carry through with them. John and Paula might be inviting in the same heartache Dan got—a pocketful of empty dreams.

She had no choice now. She'd have to grit her teeth and house two of Donovan's workers. She'd given her word to John. But she didn't have to like it. No doubt Mike Donovan had engineered this whole plot. The sooner he and his drillers were gone the better.

Cally threw the rest of the tea in the sink and went to the bedroom to dress. The sun had climbed higher, but a thick haze of milky clouds obscured it, so that it was only a silvery fish scale in the pale sky. It suited her mood just fine. In fact, if it poured rain all day, she couldn't be more pleased.

And it did pour rain. Buckets of it, accompanied by twenty-mile-per-hour winds. The first drops hit the Bucyrus Erie like a handful of rice while she was checking the drill bit, and by the time she ran back to the house she was being pelted by angry drops. John was heading back home on his tractor, and she waved halfheartedly as she went inside.

The rain slacked a bit after a couple of hours, and she

decided to take advantage of the poor weather to get some groceries.

The way things were going she expected the truck to gasp its last breath and drown in one of the pools of water along the road. She wondered how many times Daffy's brief life had passed before its headlights—visions of oil changes, tire rotations, flats, an assembly line in Detroit. She was almost home, and the truck still chugged along. A miracle. Her mood improved noticeably by the time she stopped at the house. Then the skies opened again, raining buckets while she carried the groceries in. She was drenched to the skin and shivering when she got inside. She threw the frozen food into the refrigerator and ran to the bathroom, shaking her wet clothes like a dog flinging water from its coat. She stripped quickly, shivering as drops of water from her hair fell on her bare skin. Five minutes later she was finishing a hot shower.

She slipped on the kimono and the fluffy slippers, and towel-dried her hair on her way to the kitchen. She brewed another pot of tea while she put away the rest of the groceries and the fresh pork chops from Leffert's Meat Shop. She put the box of cookies on the top shelf, where it wouldn't tempt her, then on second thought opened it and ate one. What the hell. Her size-six jeans had gotten looser since she'd been working on the drill.

She hurried to answer the tap on the door. John must have gotten caught in the downpour and doubled back for shelter.

"Hello," she called out cheerily, flinging open the door to usher him inside. Cally stopped short. Standing on her porch was Mike Donovan. Nervously she clutched her kimono about her, a sinking feeling in the pit of her stomach. He folded his umbrella and shook the water off it before he looked back at her. He was wearing a lightweight Windbreaker; it was a shade of blue that made his eyes look like sapphires. Droplets of water clung to his dark hair. "May I come in?" he asked quietly.

Cally stood aside, her thoughts in a jumble. What was he doing here?

She closed the door behind him, watching with a dry mouth as he pulled off his muddy boots and set them on the mat. He shrugged out of the Windbreaker next and laid it on the counter. Something so ordinary took on intimate meaning, and she imagined that this was what he would do first when he came home. "Is it all right if I sit down?" He was regarding her seriously, and she fought back a surge of intimidation.

"Please," she said, struggling to make her tone cool. What were the rules of etiquette when an enemy came to call? Offer him tea and cookies?

He settled himself at the kitchen table, stretching out his jean-clad legs. Helplessly her eyes followed the length of his form, coming to rest on his heavy woolen socks. Quickly she turned back to the sink and got another coffee mug from the cupboard. "Would you like something hot to drink? I can make some coffee."

"Whatever you're having's fine."

She poured him a cup of tea and set the honey on the table. Sitting down on the edge of her chair, she watched as he stirred a teaspoonful into his cup. "Rushing the season, aren't you?" he commented across the table as he held up his mug with its holly and berries.

"They were free."

He nodded. "I didn't get you up or anything, did I?"

Conscious once more of her attire, she fingered the sleeve of her kimono. "No, I just got back from the grocery store."

"If that's the mode of dress for shopping around here, this is a smaller town than I thought," Mike said.

"I got caught in the rain and took off my wet clothes," she said, stopping her halting explanation when she realized it sounded even worse.

Mike still hadn't smiled, and she couldn't detect any amusement on his face, only an intensity that puzzled her.

"And you're right about this being a small town," she said as he cupped his hands around the mug and brought it up to his sensual lips. She didn't know why she felt compelled to emphasize that fact, but it seemed important that he understand. "You can't even sneeze without Mr. Bartlett sending over cold medicine from the pharmacy."

"Meaning everyone will know about my crew staying with you and the Masterses." That was it exactly, the subject she'd skirted with her observations about the small town.

Incisively he'd gotten right to the point.

"That's right."

He set the cup down slowly before he looked at her again. "Cally, nobody's going to think anything about it. Besides, you don't strike me as the kind of woman who cares what others think." When she didn't answer, he said in a softer voice, "Happy and I are quiet and well-mannered. It'll be like having a nice old married couple staying with you."

She nearly spilled her tea. "You aren't staying here," she said adamantly. "No way. I agreed to put up some of your crew, and I'll keep my word, but it's not going to be you."

There was a long moment of silence while he watched her with glittering eyes. "Be reasonable," he said at last. "I'm not going to have those two boys staying here with you."

"Then one of the boys and Happy," she retorted.

He shook his head. "It wouldn't be fair to the boys not to let them stay together. And besides, Happy has asthma. I wouldn't trust them to help him in an emergency."

Again a thick silence engulfed them, and Cally became acutely aware of the ordinary sounds and sights of the kitchen. Her grandmother's huge gray gas stove stood against the wall, its mammoth presence cheered by two bright yellow potholders hanging from the hook on the side. A wooden mantel clock over the stove ticked by the minutes as though clucking over human waste of time. The downpour outside had lessened, and she could hear the steady drip of water from the leaky gutter on the east side. The sweet chocolaty smell of the cookies on the table mingled with the aroma of honeyed tea. The table was from her grandmother's kitchen and evoked memories of her grandparents sitting around it at night with their coffee. The bright red paint was chipped, and the metal legs scarred, and it really wasn't a pretty table, but it seemed right somehow. She ran a finger along the edge, giving herself time to manufacture some reason why Mike Donovan couldn't stay in her house.

Mike reached out and touched the brown teapot. "Somehow this doesn't seem to fit," he said.

"What?" Her startled eyes followed his hand to the teapot.

"Plain brown. I don't see you having anything plain brown. Look at this kitchen. Everywhere you have bright color. Now, that fabric picture on the wall is you." She glanced at the handmade appliqué on the wall, a picture of a barn done in red-checked gingham with green chintz hills. It was framed in an embroidery hoop. She'd finished it this past winter, working every evening with her feet propped up near the wood stove in a corner of the kitchen. "This brown teapot isn't you."

"My husband bought it," she said simply.

"I see." He was watching her.

Uneasy, she stood and rinsed out her cup in the sink. "We didn't have much money for fancy things."

"Inexpensive things don't have to be dull."

She didn't have an answer for that. What good would it do to say that Dan hadn't believed that? It would just give this man another look at her life, a life he already seemed determined to pry open despite her lack of cooperation. He caught little nuances and examined them, like a swift hand darting into a pond to come up with a tiny minnow trapped in its cupped palm.

She turned around and leaned back against the sink, curling her toes inside her fluffy slippers. He was still frowning at the brown teapot. "Where did he buy this?" he asked abruptly.

"I really don't see that that's any of your business," she said sharply.

"I was just curious," he said.

Grudgingly she shrugged. "The pharmacy. They stock a lot of odds and ends."

He hardly seemed to hear her answer, because he stood up quickly. "You know, it's not what people will think that's bothering you. It's not that at all."

"What?" She was still thinking about the teapot, and he was talking about something else.

"My staying here. It's not gossip that you're worried about."

"Oh, really? And how would you know what I think? Are you a mind reader?"

"I think I know something about you."

She bristled at his presumptuousness and put her hands

on her hips. "No, you don't."

A half-smile twisted his lips. "Yes, I do," he said softly, and his voice sent feathery shivers up her spine. He began walking toward her slowly, and Cally pressed herself against the sink, her heart thudding. Stopping a foot away from her, he studied her face until she felt he really was reading her mind. "You're not afraid of what people will think. You're afraid of me."

"That's ridiculous," she snapped, but her voice wasn't as convincing as she wished.

"Is it?" he asked mockingly. He stepped closer, until he was almost touching her, smiling when she leaned back, every muscle tensed.

"I'm not afraid of you!" Cally spoke fiercely, but her stance belied her words.

"Yes, you are," he said softly. "But more than that, you're afraid of yourself."

Now he really was ridiculous. What did she have to fear from herself?

Something altered in his face, and his voice was husky when he spoke. "You're afraid of this." He leaned closer until she could feel his warm breath on her lips. He paused fractionally, and she held her breath. His lips brushed hers, delicately at first, teasing and tempting them to open. She held them tightly closed, but after a few more feathery passes from his own firm mouth, her lips relaxed of their own volition, trembling as his assault became more demanding.

"Don't," she whispered breathlessly, but her swimming senses couldn't invest the word with any force.

He moved his head from side to side, brushing her lips lightly each time, until her eyes closed again. She was trying to reach out for one shred of sanity that would put an end to this, but her brain was as fogged in as the local airport after an early rain. Mayday. The mind has lost all instrument contact. Imminent crash.

But the warnings faded away as her lips parted, and his tongue pressed his advantage, touching sensitive recesses like lightning striking trees in a forest, leaving behind hot, sizzling sensations. Her hands had long since dropped to her sides, removing any physical barrier between them, and now he stroked her bare neck with his fingers, eliciting a low moan, half protest, half pleasure, from her. His lips meandered to her throat, nibbling until her pulse was pounding beneath his moist kisses. His fingers administered their magic lower, where her robe came together, then slipped inside and found the rounded softness of her breast. This time her moan was pure pleasure. Her hands went to his shoulders, grasping at the sinewy muscles rippling beneath her touch. "Yes," he whispered hoarsely. "Yes, Cally."

Maybe it was the sound of her name on his lips or the fact that when she opened her eyes for a moment they fell on the teapot on the table. Whatever it was, she felt a sudden flush of remorse so strong that it twisted her stomach. This was Mike Donovan touching her like this, making her respond beyond the limits of her experience. This was a stranger she mistrusted, a man who would probably hurt her. She was acting like a fool.

"No." Her own voice was small and filled with pain, and he stilled his fingers immediately.

"What is it?" he whispered, tilting her face up to look at her.

She jerked away from his touch and twisted her body from between him and the sink. "Don't do this."

He reached for her shoulders, but when she visibly stiffened he dropped his hands and followed her gaze to the teapot. "You're living in the past," he said quietly.

"No." She spun on him, her anger sparking to life. "Do you have some pat answer every time a woman says no to you? Or hasn't that ever happened before?"

From the hard glitter in his own eyes, she knew she'd succeeded in goading him to anger. "I don't make a habit of seducing women in their kitchens, if that's what you mean," he said in a low, controlled voice.

"And where do you seduce them? Their bedrooms?" She twisted her mouth in a humorless smile, and she saw his shoulders tense.

"Is that your defense, Cally—insults?" He stepped toward her, and she hastily moved back to put a kitchen chair between them. "You're afraid of what happened just now, so you're trying to drive me away with your sharp little barbs. Well, fire away, lady, because I can give as good as I get. And I won't be driven off."

"Don't you know when you've been turned down?" she snapped. "Get out of here. I'm tired of your amateur observations on my character flaws."

He pulled on the Windbreaker, his eyes never leaving her face. The ticking of the clock seemed to fill the room while he stepped into his boots, still impaling her with his steely gaze.

"You may have fooled John, but you can't fool me," she said. "You think you can weasel your way into my house, and I'll eventually fall into your arms. Well, you're wrong. Your conniving won't get you anywhere. I can't stand you."

He straightened up slowly. "For your information, I didn't trick John into giving me this drilling job and putting me up here. It was all his idea." His jaw clenched when she snorted derisively. "And you're wrong about something else, Cally Taylor. You enjoyed that kiss as much as I did." He strode out onto the porch, and Cally hurried to shut the door after him. "Happy and I'll move in tomorrow," he called as he snatched up his umbrella and ran toward his truck. Cally slammed the door with unusual force.

She braced herself the next morning when she heard a truck pull into the drive. She'd awakened early, restless. The house was cold and damp after the previous day's rain, but she finally looked at her alarm clock for the seventh time and decided that even if it was only four-thirty she might as well get up and get something done. Crawling out from under the quilt made her wish she'd just rolled over and forgotten the whole thing, but she dutifully slipped on her robe and slippers and padded to the bathroom. Even in spring, mornings were cold.

She'd done five loads of laundry the day before, but she hadn't gotten around to making up the beds in the two bedrooms yet. It seemed like an act of finality, of accepting the fact that he would be moving in. She sat in the dark in the kitchen waiting for the sun to rise, munching cookies and sipping tea. It was after the fifth cookie and second cup of tea that she decided there was no point in devastating her waistline over the matter, and she went upstairs and changed the sheets.

Now they were here, and she was determined to put on a civil front and ignore Mike as much as possible. What had happened in the kitchen yesterday had been an accident of fate. He was an attractive man. She hadn't been with a man in the year since Dan had died. It was as simple as that. And it wouldn't happen again.

She opened the door, belligerence in her stance. Mike and Happy stood on the porch, each carrying a suitcase, and Mike a small box as well. "Come on in," Cally said, stepping back.

"I told Mike we shouldn't go showing up here too early," Happy apologized, trotting in on his bowlegs and setting down his battered suitcase. "But he said you being a farmer, you was used to getting up early. And it was pretty boring hanging around that old motel room. Can't work today what with all the mud."

"Well, that about covers our morning," Mike said cheerily. "How was yours?"

"Splendid," Cally growled. "Can I get you some coffee?"

Happy's eyes lit up, but he sent a sideways look at Mike as if for permission.

"Come on in and sit down," Cally said, gesturing toward the kitchen table. In spite of everything, she liked Happy, and she wouldn't punish him just to get back at Mike. He sat down gratefully and started talking about his daughter, who was expecting a baby, and about his hunting dog Duke, who was with neighbors near St. Louis. The next thing Cally knew she'd eaten four more cookies and poured honey into another cup of tea. She could see it might be dangerous having Happy around. She could gain ten pounds just listening to his stories.

"Maybe we ought to get settled in," Mike suggested after Happy launched into a story about Duke tripping over a rabbit.

"Yeah, I'm probably boring Cally to death."

She assured him he wasn't, then led the way upstairs. She'd given Happy the room across from hers, and he thanked her profusely before ambling inside. She went on down the hall, conscious of Mike's presence right behind her, and stepped inside the bedroom. Mike looked around at the wooden floor, the braided throw rug and the oak spool bed with two handmade quilts, the top one a Log Cabin pattern. She watched the pleasure crease his face, and strangely, it pleased her as well.

He stepped over to the bed and set his suitcase on the floor, lifting his hand to trace the pattern on the quilt. "Did you make this?" he asked.

She nodded.

"You're quite handy with a needle."

Her voice was formal and stiff when she answered. "I'm not bad with pots and pans either. I majored in home ec in college."

"I didn't know you'd gone to college."

"See. You don't know me that well at all. In fact, I taught home ec in the junior high for a while."

"For a while?"

She frowned. "There was so much to do here that Dan thought . . . well, I agreed with him."

"You retired to the farm?" he asked dryly.

"I'd hardly call it retirement. Running a farm is hard work."

"Did you enjoy teaching?"

"Sure." She smiled slightly. "I enjoyed it a lot."

"Then why stay here on the farm?"

"I can't sell the farm," she explained patiently. "It was Dan's dream."

"And just because he died, you hang on to it like a ball and chain." His tone was accusing, and she paused to calm herself before answering.

"You don't understand," she said in a low voice.

"You're right. I don't."

"You and Happy share the bathroom up here," she said shortly. "I'll use the one downstairs."

She turned to go, but his voice stopped her at the door. "Here. This is for you." She stared dumbfounded as he walked toward her and held out the box he'd been carrying. She looked up at him, and he nodded. "Go ahead and take it."

"Thank you," she mumbled in confusion. Her fingers touched his as she took the box, and she tightened them automatically. Turning abruptly, she hurried down the hall, stopping at the door to her room. What had he gotten her?

She stared at the box morosely. She might as well open it. She wasn't going to divine the contents by staring through the cardboard.

Several hard tugs on the top loosened the metal staples. She pulled open the top and frowned as she looked inside. Slowly she walked to her bed and sat down. She could see a piece of china poking through some packing cardboard, and she gingerly lifted it out. She found herself staring at the Chinese teapot she'd seen in the pharmacy and desperately wanted, the one with pink roses and gold filigree. Nearly shaking in surprise, she carefully lifted out the four matching cups, tall and slender and with no handles.

"I went to the pharmacy," he said from the open door, and she turned to look at him.

"How did you know?"

"I remembered you said you got the other one there. I told the pharmacist I was looking for a teapot for you."

"Mr. Bartlett," she said, sudden comprehension dawning.

He nodded. "He said you and your husband had fought over which teapot to buy, and you finally gave in. Mr. Bartlett agreed with me. You should have this one."

"Thank you," she said softly.

"I couldn't imagine you giving in on anything," he said. "Especially on a teapot you had your heart set on."

"Sometimes you have to compromise in a good relationship," she said carefully.

Mike shook his head. "No. Sometimes one person has to give to another."

She was staring back at him, and his eyes held hers for long moments before he cleared his throat. "I'd better go get washed up."

And just like that he was gone, leaving her to trace the pink roses with her finger.

Chapter Three

CALLY WAS RINSING her breakfast dishes when Mike came into the kitchen the next morning. "There's some coffee on the stove," she said, "and cereal in the cupboard over there." She watched him from the corner of her eye as he stretched, the red flannel shirt tightening against his upper torso.

"Good morning," he murmured, his voice still husky with sleep. His hair was rumpled and his smile crooked, and Cally felt her heart do a flip-flop. In the past year, she had willed herself to forget what a pleasure it was to wake up in the morning and be joined by another human being, grumpy as Dan had normally been at this hour. She wondered if Mike was always this easygoing.

She saw his gaze move to the window above the sink, and she turned back to her dishes, flushing. The jade plant on the tiny shelf there had been replaced with the new oriental teapot and cups.

"Happy's still in bed," he said conversationally. "It's too wet to drill today, so I let him sleep. By the way, could I have a couple of eggs instead of cereal? I'll get some groceries today."

"Cooking wasn't part of the deal," she said crisply, turning from the sink. "Eggs are in the refrigerator. Now, if you'll excuse me, I have some hogs to water."

She went to the closet to get her jacket, zipping it as she started for the kitchen door. She took an inordinate amount of time putting on her gloves, watching surreptitiously as Mike, humming blithely, found a skillet on the black iron pothanger by the stove. He fished in the refrigerator and came up with two eggs, a pack of bacon, and a stick of oleo. *If he made a mess of her kitchen she'd kill him.*

She held her breath, afraid he was going to drop the eggs as he pulled a loaf of bread from the bread box. She stifled a gasp as he tripped, juggling the eggs precariously, then recovered, apparently oblivious of her presence.

He was going to make a mess. She was sure of it. She could picture everything on the floor—raw eggs, bacon, oleo, and bread—the whole works.

What was he doing now? Totally immersed in the mini-drama, she watched as he put the skillet on the front burner, then carefully laid the unopened package of bacon in the skillet. The two eggs were laid on top of that, then the stick of oleo and finally two slices of bread. Cally stared, open-mouthed.

"Do you think white wine or red would be more appropriate?" he asked, turning to her with an innocent smile.

It was a moment before it dawned on her. This whole display of male culinary ineptitude had been staged for her benefit. Mike was grinning, his eyes alight with devilish mirth.

Cally crossed her arms and sighed, an unwilling smile tugging at her mouth. "On a scale of one to ten your performance rates an eight. The stumble lacked style."

He gave a sigh of mock despondency. "Critics."

Cally hid her smile as she shut the kitchen door.

When she got back from filling the water trough, Happy was sitting at the table and Mike was serving breakfast, a large dish towel tied around his waist. Even that scene couldn't diminish his aura of raw masculinity, she thought wryly as her eyes wandered down the length of slim hips and muscled legs. She'd never seen any man wear work jeans as though they were hand-tailored.

"Morning," Happy greeted her cheerfully. "You two make me feel like an old man, snoring my head off at nine in the morning."

"You *are* an old man," Mike said. "In fact, I'm thinking of installing a rocking chair on the back of the pickup so you can supervise and rest your ancient bones at the same time."

Happy shook his head mournfully at Cally. "Watch out if he ever gives you a serious answer," he warned her.

"I've noticed he tends toward exaggeration," she observed dryly, hunting through her purse for her keys.

"Going somewhere?" Mike asked.

"To the vet's office."

"Mind if I come along? I can stop and pick up our groceries."

Cally shrugged. "It's okay with me."

She strode out the door toward her pickup, not waiting to see if he was behind her. "Cally." Her hand was on the door and she turned automatically at the sound of his voice, then chided herself for responding so quickly. "Let's take my truck."

She shook her head emphatically. "I'm in a hurry, the roads are rough, and you've got a load of casing on your truck."

He scrutinized her a moment, as though debating. Then he shrugged and climbed in the passenger side of her truck.

"Come on, Daffy," she muttered as the engine groaned. It turned over, and she pulled away.

"Daffy seems an apt name for this vehicle," Mike noted, one brow lifting as the truck backfired and lurched.

"I named it for its color, which resembled daffodils, not its temperament." She glanced at him sideways. "Otherwise, I'd have given it a male name."

"Mmmm." That dark eyebrow rose again. "What do you need at the vet's?"

"Antibiotics. The baby pigs have colds."

"Pigs catch colds?"

"They certainly do. I have sixty of them from six sows, and they're all coughing and sneezing like a roomful of first-graders in an epidemic. I bred the sows to farrow in May after the rain, but the rain came late this year." She rested her palms on the steering wheel, fingers straight in a gesture of philosophical resignation. "You can't live by the calendar."

"Is that a quote from the Farmers' Almanac?"

"I think it's a lyric from a rock song," she said wryly.

They rode in silence, if Daffy's anemic motor could be called silent. "Looks like another storm coming," Mike said, nodding toward the west, where a dark thunderhead was building on the horizon. "The forecast last night didn't say anything about rain today."

"This is western Illinois," Cally said. "There isn't a forecaster alive who can stay two steps ahead of the weather here. I hope I can give the pigs shots before it rains again." She chewed her lip worriedly, suddenly turning the truck onto a gravel road that wound its way south.

"Where are you going?" Mike demanded.

"I know a shortcut. I can get to Quincy ten minutes faster this way."

"If we aren't attacked by marauding Indians on the trail," he commented dryly.

"Stop complaining," she said. "You're going to see a famous county landmark in a minute."

"I don't believe it," Mike said a second later when the truck rounded a bend, and a wooden covered bridge loomed ahead of them.

Cally slowed the truck. "That pretty much sums up the general reaction when Oliver Zimmer built the bridge. At least that's what my grandfather told me. Zimmer came here from southeastern Pennsylvania in 1940. He was a Mennonite. He was used to covered bridges where he came from, so he built this one here over Rock Creek. This used to be his farmland." She gestured around as she started the truck slowly over the parallel slats comprising the bridge floor. The slats bumped and rumbled under the truck as they entered the wooden cavern.

"What happened to his farm?" Mike asked.

They exited the bridge, and a frown passed over Cally's face like the rain cloud now darkening the western sky. "He lost it when his corn failed the second year. My grandfather said he moved on. Went to live with a sister, I think."

"That's too bad."

"At least he left a nice bridge behind," Cally said quietly. She glanced sideways at Mike and saw him watching her with an unreadable expression, and she quickly turned back to the road, gripping the steering wheel.

"People who leave things behind don't intend for them to become monuments," he observed, his eyes narrowed. "What possessions we have on earth are temporary at best."

Cally tightened her mouth, her eyes riveted on the gravel road. "That's no reason to tear them down," she retorted fiercely. Her heart constricted. They weren't talking about the bridge now.

"I didn't say to tear it down, Cally. Just let it go."

"That's the same thing." Her knuckles were white on the steering wheel. "When you let something go, it's lost."

He didn't say anything, and when she looked at him she saw a dark, brooding look on his face. His eyes were hooded, as though his thoughts had spiraled inward. She shivered slightly. He possessed an intuitiveness capable of holding her heart up to a painfully bright light. No one had ever understood her so completely, had read her thoughts even before she spoke. Not even Dan. She felt a traitorous stab as Dan's face swam before her watering eyes.

"Look out!"

By the time she refocused her eyes, Daffy had already splashed through a puddle that felt like the Big Muddy itself. "Bull's-eye," Mike said.

"I didn't see it," Cally protested.

"You didn't notice a body of water the size of the Red Sea?"

"I'm surprised you didn't just raise your staff and part the waters," Cally muttered fractiously.

"Donovan and the Ten Commandments," he said thoughtfully, rubbing his chin. "It has possibilities."

"On second thought, you're not the Moses type. You don't have a beard."

"And what type am I?"

She gave him the benefit of a withering, cool smile. "The serpent in the Garden of Eden."

"If you'll recall, love," he said in a low voice that sent feathery shivers down her spine, "Eve succumbed to the serpent's temptation."

She was so frustrated that she slammed her fist down on the horn, and Daffy bleated like a terrorized sheep. Simultaneously the motor coughed and wheezed, and the truck rolled to a slow stop. "Now what?" Cally muttered.

"To put it in terms you'd understand, it's got water in its lungs," Mike said dryly. "Unless you're certified to perform vehicular mouth-to-mouth resuscitation, I'd say we're stranded."

"Well, do something," she cried in frustration. "Where's that spray you used the last time?"

"In my own truck," he reminded her with a lifted eyebrow. "I'm afraid the best I can do is offer my condolences."

Feeling thwarted at every turn, she hit the horn again and jumped out of the truck, slamming the door.

She heard the other door slam as she strode down the road, back toward Zimmer's Bridge, kicking at loose gravel. A moment later he caught up to her. "Wouldn't it be better to stay in the truck?" he asked with infuriating patience.

"Nobody ever uses this road. It could be days before someone came along."

He fell into step beside her, his hands jammed into his pockets. A fresh wind picked up, its cutting edge penetrating her Windbreaker. Cally pulled her collar up around her neck. The first low rumbling of thunder reached them, and Cally groaned inwardly. The sky was darkening fast. Lightning streaked overhead, and Cally ducked her head into her collar like a turtle withdrawing from the world.

"The way my luck's been going I'll probably be struck by lightning," Mike said.

"Your luck!" Cally exploded. "That's my truck sitting back there, deader than a doornail. And those are my pigs sitting at home with runny noses, waiting for antibiotics."

"And that's my head that rain's beginning to fall on," Mike added sarcastically. "I suggest we step up our pace."

She wished he'd just sprint ahead and leave her alone in the rain that had begun to fall harder, but he stuck by her side. Cally couldn't ignore the rain any longer. It was hard to ignore something that was dripping off your nose. She began to run, and Mike kept pace beside her.

She was out of breath and decidedly out of sorts when they reached the shelter of Zimmer's Bridge. She leaned her back against the bridge wall, gasping for breath. The air was heavy with the smell of damp wood. Mike was pacing, stopping occasionally to stare out at the overcast sky. Water was dripping down Cally's back, and she closed her eyes wearily. If her life were being reported play-by-play by a sportscaster, it would only be described as a series of wipeouts. *Cally comes down the hill in perfect form. Oh no, wait. She's lost her balance. She's taken a fall and she's sprawled ignomiously on the ground.* Ignominiously? Even the commentary on her life was filled with mistakes.

Mike came to a halt in front of her, studying her a moment. His voice was softer and beguiling when he spoke. "Do you know what my horoscope said today? This is a good day for physical exercise. But be sure to shower afterward."

Despite the knowledge that he was trying to coax her into a better mood, Cally began to giggle. Mike was watching her with mock sternness, and her giggles grew in force. Slowly she sank down to the floor, and leaning back, she looked up at him. "And no doubt you were born under a water sign."

He smiled down at her. "You looked like you needed cheering up."

"I did. I was just mulling over the sad state of things, Daffy in particular. And if I get bored with that, I can worry about the pigs or the cattle or the price of corn. Why, if I want to, I can even worry about what the market prices will be in a few months. That's a real downer." Why was she babbling on? She didn't want him to feel sorry for her.

What did she want? She wanted him to stop looking at her the way a man looks at a woman, a look that was open and decidedly masculine and wrapped itself around her like an embrace.

He sank down beside her, and for a while they sat silently, listening to the rain pelt the roof. The proximity of his leg to hers was making her pulse race in tandem with Rock Creek, which bubbled over the stones beneath them. Daffy was a pale yellow speck a quarter mile up the road, looking abandoned and forlorn.

The rain slacked to a steady drizzle, running down the gravel road in rivulets. A rut was developing near the side of the road as the rivulet wore through to the gray clay base. It seemed like everything wore through around here. Her fences, the fields, the house, and even her life.

"How do you do it every day?" Mike asked suddenly, and she turned her head in confusion.

"Do what?"

"Work so hard, just survive. How do you get through each day?"

"I try not to think about that," she said wryly. "Actually the farm is my reason for being. It's an effort to keep it going, but I don't know what else to do."

"Sell it," he said with the voice of authority.

"I already told you I can't do that. Let's not fight about it again."

He shrugged. "You need to be with people more. You're not the kind of woman who should be locked away like a nun."

"Very few nuns run Bucyrus Eries," she informed him. "Besides, I have enough of a social life. There's the drive-in and the diner and my 4-H club."

"You're a 4-H'er?" he asked, grinning.

"Head, heart, hands, and health," she replied solemnly, holding up her hand. "I've got ten girls in my club."

"Now *that* I can picture," he said. "You're probably very good at teaching them how to bake cookies and sew quilts."

"Pincushions," she said, smiling. "They're little girls."

He was sitting close to her, so close she could see each droplet of rain still clinging to his dark hair. His eyes roved over her face, and what she saw there stirred something deep inside her. She had thought a part of her had died with Dan, but she could feel it awakening, brought back to life by that expression in Mike's face. Her mouth opened slowly, but she didn't know what it was she was going to say. It was something fleeting, almost indefinable. She shivered, and instantly his hand touched her damp hair.

"You're cold," he said softly. His hand trailed down her cheek, and it seemed to her that his touch was more than flesh against flesh. She came to life wherever his fingers gently explored. Her eyes were riveted on his face, her breath suspended.

He cupped her face. Her heart was pounding so hard it took her breath away. Heat suffused her body and ran through her veins like a river of warm honey, thick and sweet. She sucked in air raggedly, startled by the powerful emotions churning inside her. It was truly an awakening, because she'd never in her life felt like this before.

He murmured her name, his lips touching hers like a breeze caressing silk. Pliant yet hungry, her mouth opened beneath his, wanting his touch. She reached up and covered his hands where they rested on her face, pressing their warm, healing touch against her starving flesh.

"Touch me," he whispered, gently taking her hand and slipping it inside his Windbreaker and shirt, pressing it against his heart. She could feel it pounding in a rhythm that matched her own frenzied pulse. "It's not Zimmer's Bridge making it do that," he whispered. "It's you, Cally."

She left her hand there even when he released it and cradled her head to his shoulder. The rain had stopped, and the soft chirr of young frogs floated on the air. Through his encircling arms she could see the road beyond the bridge, the air misty, as though hung with tiny pearls of dew, the grass a newly washed green. Everything was alive and new, and it was one of those rare moments when she felt at peace with the world.

His head bent lower and planted soft, fervent kisses on her neck. Cally tilted up her face, offering her throat to his warm ministrations, her black hair cascading down her back. She laced her fingers behind his neck and drew him even closer. Her mouth parted on a sigh of pleasure as his teeth nibbled teasingly up her neck and back to her earlobe. "You're so soft and sweet," he whispered against her ear. Slowly he began unbuttoning her blouse. His fingers played gently inside its folds, tantalizing rosy nipples into hardened peaks.

Instinctively she knew that another minute of his tender assault and she would be lost to him. A memory stirred dimly in the back of her mind, and she struggled to bring it into focus. Outside, a crow cawed as he flapped down to drink from the creek, and a sharp recollection pierced Cally's consciousness. Crows had been feeding in the cornfield the day the driller had made a pass at her, and their cries had mingled with her own angry words.

Mike's promise that day in the diner made her face burn. *If the opportunity presents itself* . . . Here she sat in Zimmer's Bridge, half dressed, entwined in the embrace of a man who was out to bed her. The rain must have soaked her brain.

Pulling away from him, she leaped to her feet and half-

ran for the road, emerging from the darkened bridge into
hazy sunshine.

She was fumbling with her blouse, having little success
buttoning it while she walked rapidly, when he caught up
to her. "What's wrong?" he demanded.

She rounded on him furiously. "Nothing's wrong," she
spat out, her voice rising an octave. "I make an appointment
at least once a year to get together with a man in Zimmer's
Bridge—sort of a checkup for my libido."

"Let me do that," he muttered, brushing her agitated
hands aside and efficiently buttoning her blouse. His voice
was exasperated and gentle at the same time, like steel and
velvet. "I hope you don't think that what happened in there
is the same as some back-alley tryst between strangers."

"Back alley, the inside of a bridge—what's the difference? And we *are* strangers."

Mike took a deep breath and expelled it slowly, falling
into step beside her as she trudged on up the road. "I'm
sorry I rushed you," he said, jamming his hands into his
pockets. "I keep forgetting we've just met. I feel like I've
known you all my life, feel like I've been waiting for you."

His voice was soft and distant as he said the last, and
she dared a sideways glance at his face. Again, he'd masked
it, staring off into the distance as though she no longer
walked beside him. Cally frowned and mulled over his words.
It was just a line, the kind of thing all men said when they
wanted something. Mike Donovan was smooth—she
wouldn't forget that again—and he was the most attractive
man she'd ever met. But from now on she was going to
cultivate a strong immunity to his charms.

At least the rest of the morning was characterized by
some degree of efficiency. Happy chortled over Daffy's
drowning, that is until Mike threw him a black look. Together the three of them rode back in Mike's truck to the
scene of Daffy's demise. After a certain amount of work
under the hood with the spray, accompanied by an equal
amount of muttering from Mike, the truck started. Happy
drove it back to the farm, while Cally and Mike went into
town in his truck.

The first stop was the vet's office for antibiotics. Now

Cally pushed the grocery cart down the aisles of the Bi-Rite store while Mike inspected the shelves, methodically pitching cans of chili and soup into the cart. Cally had picked out a jar of olives, her weakness.

"I think you have a tin fetish," Cally observed. "You haven't gotten anything yet that grows in the ground."

"Spoken like a true farmer," he said, flourishing a can of tuna before he added it to the growing pile in the cart.

"Don't you ever eat real food?"

"Sure. In fact, I'm a nut for pasta." Mike harvested a bundle of spaghetti packages from the top shelf and deposited them in the cart.

"What are you going to put on that spaghetti—tuna?"

"Infidel," he said with a mournful shake of his head.

"Now, personally, I like Mexican food," Cally said, eyeing the boxes of taco shells.

"And what do you put in them?" Mike asked, tossing a box in the cart. "Olives?"

"Now you've thrown down the gauntlet," Cally said. "I'll match my tacos against your pasta any day."

"All right, you're on. This week we hold the Great American Drillers Cookoff."

The challenge issued, Cally joined the shopping with new fervor, pondering over ripe avocados and sour cream and Cheddar cheese.

"Vass ist das?" Mike said, hefting a cabbage. "Ja, die cabbage. Now, mit die cabbage vee make die slaw or die kraut. Kraut und sausage, wunderbar."

Cally eyed him askance. "You look like a ventriloquist with his dummy."

Mike lowered the cabbage and cradled it in his arm. "Mein herr," he said in a formal, clipped accent, "how is the weather?"

Lowering his voice to a husky growl, his lips barely moving, he answered, "S'alright."

Giggling, Cally said, "I bet you can't make him talk while you drink a glass of water."

"No, but he can drink a glass of water while I talk."

She was laughing harder, and when she looked around she saw Jimmy, Bi-Rite's vegetable handler, staring at them, his mouth agape. He was spraying the fresh vegetables with water, but he was so intent on Cally and Mike that he'd directed the nozzle onto the floor instead of the broccoli. Cally dissolved in fresh gales of laughter as the water pooled around Jimmy's shoes.

"I always like an appreciative audience," Mike said, putting the cabbage back in the bin.

Cally was still suppressing giggles as they wheeled the cart past Jimmy, now frantically mopping up water with a roll of paper towels. When they were around the corner and out of earshot, Cally whispered, "I bet he hasn't been that entertained since Mrs. Chumley caught her wig on a pineapple when she bent over to smell the grapefruit. She was always accusing Jimmy of putting old grapefruit on top."

At the checkout Mike insisted on paying, though Cally protested that at least a third of the groceries were hers. "I'll help you eat them," Mike assured her.

She continued to argue during the trip home, insisting that he understand the arrangement—their groceries were to remain separate, and she would pay for hers.

"Short of building a wall down half the refrigerator, I don't see how that can work," he observed.

"I know what you're trying to do, but I can afford to pay for my own groceries."

Mike sighed. "Cally, I know what it's like to try to work a farm. Profits are nearly nonexistent. I've done a lot of drilling in rural areas, and I've seen good people work themselves to death."

Cally tightened her lips. "I don't want your money, Mike."

"I'm no threat to your independence, Cally. Really. What I had in mind was different. I'm offering you a job."

"A job?" She stared at him in surprise.

"Why don't you help me on my drill rig? I'll pay you by the hour, same as I pay Happy and the boys, and you'll still have time to take care of the farm."

"Pay me for what?" she asked coolly. "For fetching you water and brewing your coffee?"

Mike shook his head with a quick, irritated motion. "No, of course not. Anyone who can operate an old Bucyrus Erie can operate a hydraulic rig. Happy and I can do the heavy work, like setting casing, but otherwise you'd be an equal."

"An equal," she fumed. "I see what you're doing, Mike

Donovan, and it won't work. You figure you can bribe me with some easy money and keep me from operating the Bucyrus Erie. I just bet you'd let me do everything but set casing. I don't want a handout, so just forget it. I don't have any intention of giving up the Bucyrus Erie."

"Damn it, Cally! You're the most exasperating woman I ever met. Why can't you be reasonable?"

"I'm not unreasonable. You are." She crossed her arms and stared out the window. She heard Mike emit a low growl of frustration under his breath, and the rest of the ride was completed in silence.

The sun shone brightly the next morning, and the breeze was brisk. Cally had run a hose to the hog trough. The pigs looked decidedly better since she'd given them antibiotic shots yesterday. She heard the motor start on the Donovan Drilling rig on George Fanning's land, and a few minutes later the red truck topped the hill at the end of the field. Hastily Cally went into the farrowing house until the rig and pickup had passed through on their way to a drilling spot on John's land.

Mike and Happy had spent the better part of yesterday evening preparing to move the drilling rig to John's property. Mike said he planned to have the two boys set up on George Fanning's new drill site when the second boy arrived from St. Louis with the rig. Mike had been courteous to her that night, but certainly not overly warm. Happy carried most of the conversation at dinner. Mike had briefly stated that she was being ridiculous, insisting on eating a cold salad with cheese when he was frying hamburgers, but he hadn't pressed the issue. Unfortunately for Cally, the aroma of hamburgers hung in the house all night, and she mentally cursed Mike while she lay in bed listening to her stomach growl.

Cally started walking back to the house, rubbing her eyes sleepily. Between her stomach's protests and Happy's buzz-saw snoring, she hadn't slept well last night. The fact that she was feeling churlish this morning was partly due to her fitful sleep and partly due to the cheerful, almost maniacal smile Mike gave her as he piled pancakes on his plate and

Happy's, while Cally halfheartedly munched cereal.

She drew up short when she saw the canary-yellow pickup truck sitting next to Daffy. For a minute she thought she was seeing double, but on closer inspection it was obvious that the new truck lacked certain things that Daffy possessed—rust spots, bald tires, and chipped paint. For a wild moment she imagined that perhaps Daffy had bred with that nice Mack truck she'd parked next to at the diner last week, and the result was this bouncing baby pickup. But then sanity prevailed.

Tentatively she approached the truck and ran her hand over its glossy exterior. The front sported an antenna, and she peered inside for the radio. Talk about class—not only a radio but a tape deck as well. This had to be Mike's truck. Even the seed dealers who occasionally called on her didn't drive new pickups. The keys were sitting on the front seat, on top of a piece of paper. Cally tried to read the paper through the glass, then gave in to curiosity and opened the door, sliding into the driver's seat and reveling in the luxurious feel of new upholstery. Poor Daffy's seat was so battered that a spring had worn through, and it poked her thigh each time she moved her leg to put in the clutch.

She pushed aside the keys and picked up the paper. Quickly she scanned it, and then she read it again more slowly. It was the title to the truck, and it was in her name.

There had to be some mistake. She could never afford a truck like this. Whatever was going on, she had a feeling that Mike Donovan was behind it.

Cally tapped her foot on the kitchen floor while she dialed the Ford dealership. "Harley Ferguson, please," she told the receptionist. She and Harley had gone to high school together.

"Harley, this is Cally Taylor. What's that yellow truck doing sitting in my driveway?"

"Well, hi, Cally. How's it going?"

"Not well, Harley. Not well at all. There's a truck in my drive that I didn't order and can't pay for. Now that's a problem, Harley."

"Now, Cally, don't go getting upset." Harley's slow drawl reminded Cally of how long he used to take to get out an answer in high school history class, and she found her foot tapping faster.

"I'm not upset," she said through gritted teeth. "I'm past that, Harley. Does the word apoplectic mean anything to you?"

"I'm sorry if your hogs are sick again, Cally, but don't let it get you down."

Her toes curled tightly as she struggled to suppress a frustrated scream. She should have remembered that Harley was almost as good in vocabulary as he was in history.

"Never mind my hogs. What about the truck?"

"It's yours."

"If you could see my bank statement you wouldn't make such a ludicrous remark. I can't afford a new truck."

"It's all paid for. Fellow name of Mike Donovan came in yesterday afternoon late and paid cash. Said to take the truck over to your house today. Had a devil of a time getting a bright yellow one for him too. I finally had one brought over from Hannibal."

"Thanks, Harley," she said with icy calm. "That's all I needed to know."

"Listen, Cally, we didn't have time to do the under-coating. Bring it in whenever you get the time and we'll take care of it."

"Oh, everything's going to be taken care of just fine," she said with acid sweetness. "Good-bye, Harley."

Cally set to work on the Bucyrus Erie, one eye on the derrick of the Donovan drill rig, which poked up over the trees behind John's house. She was waiting for Mike Donovan the way the barnyard cat waited for a mouse at the grain bin, tail twitching, eyes glittering. The minute he showed his face Cally was going to pounce.

It was difficult to get any work done with such a short attention span, so the morning was unfruitful. Noon came, and she strained for sounds of his approaching truck. Noon went, and still she stared off into the distance, waiting. Finally she went back to work.

The rig was ready to drill, and Cally held her breath as she started the engine on the back of the rig, then put it in gear. Slowly and steadily, the cable worked up and down, pounding the drill bit into the hard earth. It was working! She actually had the old rig drilling. It would probably take a month or more on this hole, but she was sure at this moment that she would hit oil.

The afternoon wore on, and Cally was lulled into a sense of well-being by the steady rhythm of the drill. The engine hummed and rocked as the machine drilled, and she sat down to rest.

Every five feet she had to stop the drill, pull out the cable, and lower the bail bucket into the hole to haul out the cuttings. Cuttings were the bits of rock and dirt left in the hole by the drill's action, and they had to be brought to the surface and disposed of. Cally had already prepared a large hole near the drill, and she emptied the bail bucket into the hole.

The drill was humming again, going *ker-chunk, ker-chunk,* as dusk fell. A sliver of moon topped the trees, and Cally saw John's yard light go on. She stood up, wondering if Mike was finally heading back. At the same time there was a terrible crunching sound, and the Bucyrus Erie shuddered, and in the instant that she realized what was happening, the cable lost all tension and flew free, up in the air. Cally ran to shut down the drill, but the damage had been done. Her bit was gone. Damn.

The bit had lodged in a hard layer of Kinderhook shale. The cable was old and weak, and it had caught in the shale, breaking off. Now her bit was down in the hole, and she'd have to fish it out.

She glared up at the moon, as if it had some hand in this fiasco. At that moment a more suitable target for her wrath presented himself. The red pickup came up the road and turned into her drive. Her frustration with the drill transferred itself to Mike Donovan, and his gift of the truck took on new proportions.

She stalked toward the house, her long hair blowing in the breeze, her anger mounting with every step. The lights were on in the kitchen when she opened the door, and Mike turned from the sink where he was washing his hands. His eyes made a quick assessment of her, and she saw his shoulders tense. "Apparently my hope that you would cool down if I stayed away all day has been dashed," he said quietly.

"Damn right," she muttered, planting her feet and glaring at him. "Just what was the big idea of giving me a new truck?"

He carefully dried his hands before speaking. "I considered several ways of doing this, Cally. I had planned to tell you it was a company truck that you could use, but you refused to work for me. I even considered hiring someone to show up here and announce that you'd won it in a sweepstakes, but I figured you're not the kind of person who enters sweepstakes. So I took the only other option. I simply bought the truck and left it here for you to find. I really thought you'd be calmer by now."

"No, you didn't think," she accused him. "It didn't matter to you that I feel bad because I can't afford a new truck. You expected me to fall over you with gratitude, and I can't do that, Mike. Because this is a matter of pride. If I accepted this truck, then I'd owe you. And I won't do that."

Mike threw the hand towel down on the counter, his eyes blazing. "Is your pride going to get you home safely, Cally, when that broken-down rattletrap of yours quits again in the middle of God knows where? Is your pride going to haul supplies from the store? Is your pride going to keep you from getting hurt when one of those paper-thin tires blows on the highway?"

Tears were welling in her eyes. "No," she said. "It's not going to get me anything. But pride's all I've got right now. And I can't let you take that from me."

She turned on her heel and ran for the stairs. A startled Happy murmured hello when she passed him, and Cally choked out an answer before she reached the sanctity of her bedroom. She closed the door and threw herself across her bed, the tears flowing.

Chapter Four

CALLY SAT AT the kitchen table the next morning, swirling her spoon in her oatmeal. She fished out a piece of chopped date and popped it in her mouth, sucking on it. The veil of night was lifting, and the gray sky flushed pink as a young girl's cheeks while the sun rose. Dew still clung to the grass and to the lacy spider webs woven between individual blades. Overnight, it seemed, the first crimson blossoms had burst forth on the redbud tree. This morning it didn't particularly cheer her.

The floor squeaked upstairs, and she stiffened. She could run outside and start working before Mike came down, but it was her house and she wasn't going to hide from him. If he wanted to make an issue of the truck again today, she would refuse to listen.

She heard his soft tread on the steps and hastily went back to her oatmeal, making an undue amount of noise with the spoon. His footsteps stopped outside the kitchen door, and after several long moments of silence Cally looked up. Mike was out of sight, but poking into the kitchen was a wooden coat hanger with a white handkerchief tied to the end. It was slowly waving back and forth. Cally made a choking sound in her throat, and Mike poked his head around the doorframe. "Truce?" he asked softly with that characteristic raise of an eyebrow.

"You have a demented sense of humor," she groused, trying to hide her smile.

He ventured into the kitchen, still holding his flag aloft. "That must be what attracts you to me," he said confidently.

"I think you have that backward."

"Another of my endearing qualities—slight confusion."

"You're about as confused as my calculator," Cally said, watching as he helped himself to some cereal. He sat down opposite her, offering her a boyish smile, and Cally sighed as the scent of his cologne reached her. How could any man slicing bananas into a bowl of chocolate-flavored cereal look so devastating at this hour of the morning? It was impossible to stay mad at him.

"Am I forgiven?" he asked, slanting her a crooked smile.

Cally tried to look stern and failed miserably. Her heart wasn't in it. "This time," she said grudgingly.

"Good. Then I'm taking you out in our new truck tonight as a peace offering."

"*Our* new truck?"

"To avoid future arguments, I suggest we share ownership. And our first order of business is to give it a proper name."

"Should we send out birth announcements?" Cally asked dryly.

Ignoring her gibe, he frowned thoughtfully. "Sunshine? Let's see. What else is yellow? Lemon? No, that might be tempting the fates."

Cally began to see possibilities in this. "Considering we're co-owners, I think it ought to be named after a battlefield. It hasn't exactly been a symbol of tranquillity."

"You're right," Mike said, staring into space as he crunched his cereal. "How about Gettysburg? No, too pretentious."

"I've got it," Cally said. "Bunker Hill. It has a certain aristocratic flair, don't you think?"

"That's it," Mike agreed. "We can call it Bunky for short. Now where can we go tonight to celebrate? How about a movie?"

"All we have here is the drive-in, unless you want to drive all the way to Quincy."

"The drive-in sounds fine. We can go right after dinner." Mike glanced at his watch. "I'd better go wake Happy. Although I'm probably taking my life in my hands. He chewed me out royally last night for upsetting you."

"He's a sweet old man," Cally said, smiling.

"No he isn't. He's an old mule with a burr under his collar, and he said that if I make you cry again he's going to drop a load of casing on my head." Mike stood up and stared balefully toward the stairs. "Maybe I ought to carry my white flag."

"Go get him, soldier," Cally said, carrying her bowl to the sink.

She was pulling on her sweater when she heard a loud thump upstairs, a sound not unlike a shoe hitting a wall. "Simmer down, you old goat! She's not mad at me anymore." The next sound was Mike's voice carrying down the hall.

Cally smiled and went out the door.

Apparently the men had taken sandwiches with them, because they didn't return for lunch. Cally spent the better part of the morning searching the farm for the fishing tool needed to retrieve the bit from the hole. After a thorough but fruitless three hours in the main barn, tool shed, and old milk house—and a long discussion with Fearless, her tabby, about the two mice she'd seen in the granary—she found the tool in the garage, beside the lawn mower. "Not bright, Cally," she muttered.

She broke for lunch, then whiled away the afternoon retying the cable and attaching the spearlike fishing tool with barbs on the side for snagging the bit. It was late afternoon, and she was tired.

She lowered the cable into the hole and engaged the gear, holding the cable as it moved up and down, hoping to feel a catch as it snagged the broken cable attached to the bit in the hole. Another hour passed that way.

Maybe Mike was right, she thought in despair as she sat down on the ground to rest. She ought to help him on his rig and forget about the Bucyrus Erie. She rubbed her temples and glanced around. The daffodils were fading, their flower heads pale and drooped, like old crepe paper. Soon they'd be replaced by the flowers of summer—marigolds, petunias, and phlox.

She watched as a young heifer cavorted along the fence, kicking up its rear hooves and bucking for the sheer joy of it. What magic was there in spring air that made the blood boil? Whatever, it was in Mike's eyes and touch. The poignancy was in the fleeting pleasure. Spring would give way to the heat of summer just as winter's pall hung on the heels of autumn. And what hung on the heels of Mike Donovan's heated glance—a winter of another sort after he tired of the look and feel of her?

One thing you understood when you lived on a farm was cycles. Things bloomed and faded, died and seeded again. She was completing a cycle begun by her grandfather with the Bucyrus Erie, and she was continuing a cycle begun by Dan. She knew that the cycle wouldn't be complete until she'd realized their dreams—until she found oil. But that sounded stupid and hardheaded when she tried to say it out loud. It was something she couldn't say to Mike. And now their two circles had crossed and clashed, his life and hers.

Sighing, she turned back to the drill. Well, as Donna was fond of saying, if life were easy, there'd be no need for deodorant. Probably only Donna knew what that meant.

She was spattered with mud and grease, and her hair had blown into a wild mane by the time Mike's pickup turned into the drive early that evening. He hopped out, and Happy drove on to the house. "How are you doing?" he called.

"Not well," Cally said when he reached her side. He brushed back a piece of her hair and rubbed some grease off her forehead with his thumb. "You look like you've been rolling in the mud," he commented.

"I've been trying to get the bit out of the hole. The cable broke."

Mike whistled softly. "You must have had a rough day, honey. Here, let me take a look." Cally watched him as he walked to the Bucyrus Erie and checked the cable.

She plucked a blade of grass and sucked on it while he worked. His arm muscles knotted against his shirt, and

Cally's eyes roved hungrily on down to his thighs, corded and strong as they strained against the fabric of his jeans. He was absorbed in the cable, the planes of his face thrown into dusky light and shadow by the setting sun. His hair blew casually in the dying breeze. His hands looked capable and strong as he worked the cable, and Cally swallowed as she remembered their touch on her skin. She felt such a tug on her heart that she turned away, taking a deep breath and focusing on the last purple rays of the setting sun as they touched the edge of her field. When she was little, her mother used to say that when sunlight touched the earth in a single ray like that it was an angel blessing the place.

"I think I've got it," Mike said triumphantly, and Cally turned back to him. He raised the cable slowly and hauled the bit out of the hole, dropping it on the ground. He shook his head. "That was a bit of good luck getting it back. Want me to put it back on line for you?"

"That can wait until tomorrow," Cally pronounced. "I'm going to the drive-in tonight. And as payment for your hard work I'll buy the tickets."

"Your generosity knows no bounds." Mike grinned. "Let's get cleaned up and eat some dinner."

Happy was decidedly—well, happy—that they were going out, and he hummed and did a little jig as he served the chili. Cally grabbed for her glass of soda after that first bite, and Mike laughed. "I told you your cooking would rot the innards of a metal pipe," he told Happy, his eyes sparkling.

"It's fine," Cally gasped. "Really delicious. What's in here?" She had a suspicion it was propane fuel.

Happy beamed. "I just took a can of chili and doctored it up a bit with some tabasco, cumin, coriander, and chili peppers."

Cally nodded, unable to speak. Her eyes were watering.

"See what you've done with that high-octane mess," Mike chided Happy. "Now Cally's breath'll fog up the truck windows."

"You just be sure she has a good time," Happy retorted.

Mike sat back and grinned, winking at Cally.

Mike insisted they christen the new truck, so with Happy looking on, shaking his head, Cally poured a bottle of root

beer over the fender and dubbed the truck Bunky. Happy
was standing in the drive, his thumbs hooked in the top of
his overalls, still shaking his head as they pulled away.

"This is luxurious," Cally murmured, running her hand
over the new upholstery. "It feels strange not to have my
leg battling with a spring."

Mike turned to look at her, and the light in his eyes made
her heart beat faster. "I think there must be something wrong
with this truck," she said nervously. "The engine doesn't
make any noise." She lowered her eyes, fingering the seat.

"You look beautiful tonight," Mike said softly.

She smiled at him tentatively and turned her gaze to the
passing scenery, feeling awkward because of these strange
palpitations she was experiencing.

It must have been a year since she had worn anything
but jeans, and that had been at Dan's funeral. Self-consciously, she smoothed her skirt. It was cut full, bright red
with a ruffle at the hem. She'd put on a red and navy blue
striped blouse and gold clip earrings. Her black hair was
smoothed back and anchored at her nape with a comb, a
few stray tendrils framing her face. A little blusher and
mascara served to accent the natural glow of her skin.

She handed him the two dollars admission, and his hand
tightened over hers for a moment. Cally saw Nona, the
ticket clerk, give Mike the once-over, then peer past him
at Cally.

Mike parked the truck beside a speaker and gazed around
in apparent bewilderment as horns honked and waving arms
emerged from windows. A few heads poked out and stared
at the yellow truck. "Is everyone paying an unusual amount
of attention to our arrival, or am I imagining things?" Mike
asked.

Cally laughed. "The drive-in just opened for the season
tonight. Everyone's here to see who's necking with whom."
Catching the amused raise of an eyebrow, she belatedly
tried to explain herself. "I mean, who's dating . . ." She felt
a warm flush creeping up her face, and she cleared her
throat. "That chili sure was hot."

Mike grinned at her, and she gave him a wan smile.
"Maybe we ought to check out the speaker," she suggested,

but still he smiled at her another long minute before he turned his attention to the black object outside. He hung it on the window and turned on the volume control. The local radio station came on, then faded in and out with depressing regularity. "I've never seen one of these that worked right," Mike said. "I think drive-in gremlins come through at night and loosen strategic nuts and bolts."

"Well, at least the cord reaches far enough," Cally said. "They often don't, you know."

"Hey, Cally," a male voice called from a nearby car. "Who's the guy you roped into taking you to the movies?"

"No one you'd know, Jackson," she called back. "He's not a hog farmer or a hog."

"That's telling him, Cally," a girl called from another car.

"Is he a rejected suitor?" Mike asked.

"He was a friend of Dan's," Cally said evasively.

She could feel Mike scrutinizing her. "But not yours?"

"Jackson's a bit of a showoff. He used to come by the farm a lot. I always got the distinct impression he came to gloat over how well he'd done in his father's insurance business. But Dan held him up as a shining example, a local boy who made good."

"And after Dan died?"

"My, but we're inquisitive tonight," she said tartly.

"I got the impression your dislike of Jackson is on a more personal level."

"What sharp ears you have, Grandma," she said with a tight smile. "As a matter of fact, Jackson did come around after Dan died. To console the grieving widow. And see if she was interested in a little hanky-panky after the funeral."

She glanced at Mike and saw his jaw tighten. "Too bad he's not parked closer," he muttered.

"Don't worry. I poured a vase of flowers over his head."

Horns began honking all around as the screen flickered and came to life. "By the way," Mike said. "What are we seeing tonight?"

"I think it's *The Possum That Ate Toledo*."

"Oh, good. A foreign film." Cally laughed.

"Come here, you," Mike growled, pulling her against him, his arm on her shoulder. "All this talk about possums is making me romantic."

Cally smiled and leaned her head on his shoulder as his arm tightened around her. The movie turned out to be one of those beach pictures where all the males had surfboards and the girls ran around in halter tops oohing and ahhing. It held their interest for all of five minutes.

Mike's fingers were gently playing over Cally's shoulder. "How did your husband die?" he asked abruptly, and the way he asked it Cally was sure he'd been thinking about Dan for some time.

"He was killed in an accident. A tractor rolled over on him."

"I'm sorry. He must have been quite young."

"Young and old at the same time," Cally said. "The farm aged Dan. That and . . . well, just the farm." She'd started to mention the drillers who'd taken his money, but she caught herself in time.

She felt Mike's fingers tighten almost imperceptibly. "Were you happy?"

"We were—" she began, then stopped and turned to look at him, frowning. "I don't want to talk about this with you."

"Cally." His blue eyes were pensive, but whatever he had been about to say died on his lips. His gaze riveted hers. He half-turned her to him, his fingers pressing her back, drawing her closer. He whispered her name again, and this time his voice was hungry. His gaze seemed to devour her, and Cally felt an answering hunger. She closed her eyes heavily as he tilted her chin up and his breath touched her cheek. He was so filled with life, she thought, distracted, as his firm lips claimed her own. The sweet scent of his clean shirt mingled with his own musky scent, and Cally drank in every detail with her senses.

"Hi, Cally." She jumped back from Mike, her eyes flying open. Over his shoulder she could see nine-year-old Bix Allen, his arms crossed on the door as he stared in at them. Mike sighed and fixed a pained smile on his face as he swung around to the boy.

"Would you like to earn a quarter, young man?" he asked with the patience of a man near the point of creative murder.

"Why don't you go count how many people are in each car here tonight?" He dug in his pocket and handed Bix a quarter.

Bix shrugged and examined the quarter. Then he glanced back at Cally with businesslike aplomb. "My sister said to tell you she can't make cookies for the next 4-H meeting. Mom's pot roast caught the oven on fire."

"Fine, Bix," Cally said, her hands fluttering around her hair. "I'll take care of the cookies."

"Okay." He stood where he was, seemingly content to look them over.

"Don't you have a census to take, Bix?" Mike prompted him.

"Huh? Oh, yeah, sure. See you later."

He stepped away from the truck, and Mike slowly turned back to Cally. "Now, where were we?"

She planted her arms around his neck and pulled him to her. "Right in the middle of this." His eyes sparkled with mirth as he lowered his head to hers.

"Why, Mike, what a surprise to see you here."

There was no mistaking that seductive drawl, Cally thought with an inward groan.

"Reba," Mike said, rolling his eyes skyward. Fixing that same wooden smile on his face he turned to her. "What are you doing here?"

"I'm here with Joe. I was just on my way to get some popcorn when I thought I recognized you." She glanced at Cally, and Cally gave her a weak wave. "Well, see you two," Reba said, snapping her chewing gum as she sauntered off.

"Who's Joe?" Mike asked between gritted teeth as he turned back to Cally. "Nice of her to stop by to tell us about it."

"Joe washes dishes at Gordon's," Cally explained. She sighed. "You know, we might as well watch the movie. There's no end to the number of people here tonight who might know me."

"You're probably right," Mike said, disengaging his arm from her shoulder. He heaved a deep sigh. "Want some popcorn?"

Cally grinned at him. "With extra butter. And a chocolate bar."

* * *

The moon rode high over the redbud when the truck pulled into Cally's driveway later that night. "Looks like Happy is up late reading another detective novel," Mike said, nodding toward the light in the upstairs window. He turned off the engine and leaned back, closing his eyes. When he opened them and looked at Cally, she was drawn into their blue, tantalizing depths.

His fingers moved restlessly over her throat, shoulders, and face, touching her mouth into stillness when she parted her lips to speak. "Shhh," he murmured softly, and he touched her mouth lightly with his own, then brushed it over and over, his lips more demanding each time, as though the friction sparked a need he couldn't satisfy.

Gently he removed the comb from her hair and allowed his lean fingers to play through her thick mane. He buried his mouth against her neck, holding a fistful of her silky black hair against his face. He sighed raggedly. "You're so beautiful," he whispered. "I hope you were happy."

It took a moment before his words sank in. "What?" she murmured in confusion.

Slowly he lifted his head and searched her face. "I hope you and Dan were happy. It would hurt to think of you unhappy, even with someone else."

Her mouth moved shakily. She searched for the right words. Dan's face was clouding her thoughts, and she shook her head briefly to clear her mind. "We'd better go in," she said at last, not wanting him to say any more.

Mike's eyes still held hers. "If you ever want to talk, I'm here, Cally. Just tell me."

She busied herself by picking up the empty popcorn box and the candy wrappers. "I guess I'm a little tired tonight," she said with a weak smile. "I'd better go to bed." She slid out of the truck, conscious of him watching her. She didn't want to think about his question tonight. It had brought back painful memories. When he first asked if she had been happy, surprising her with his usual bluntness, she had almost blurted out that she and Dan had been content, comfortable with each other. She had stopped herself in time, but the question had haunted her all evening. At the time she had supposed that comfortable was the same thing as happy. But Mike's unsettling presence was making her question a lot of things she had once simply accepted.

He opened the kitchen door for her, and after a hasty good-night Cally went upstairs to bed. Her head was hurting with the effort of trying not to think about Dan. She kept seeing his face but hearing Mike's voice. It frightened her that she couldn't remember exactly how Dan had sounded.

The following day, Saturday, was the day Cally and Mike had designated the Great American Drillers Cookoff, and starting at two in the afternoon they both bustled around the kitchen. After half an hour of lighthearted bickering over rights to the work space, they set a row of cans down the center of the counter and retired to their respective battle stations.

A brash male cardinal took up a position in the redbud outside the kitchen window and began claiming his own territory, singing at the top of his lungs. Mike was busy stirring some kind of sauce for spaghetti, and he joined the cardinal with his own rendition of "Arrivederci, Roma." He had a rich bass voice, but he sang with an exaggerated accent, and Cally retaliated by whistling the Mexican Hat Dance, thumping the wooden cabinet at the proper rhythm points. They both started laughing when the cardinal gave up and flew away.

"The only thing better than laughter in the kitchen," Mike said, "is kissing." He gave her a quick peck on the cheek, then murmured, "Mmmm," and came back for more. Sweeping her into his arms, he bent her back and gave her a deep kiss that made her head reel.

Happy entered the kitchen just then, and Cally straightened abruptly. "I won't even ask," he muttered as Cally and Mike burst into fresh peals of laughter.

They began putting their creations on the table, lining them up like entries at the county fair. Cally set down bowls of taco shells and assorted condiments, watching from the corner of her eye as Mike brought forth a fancy dish of pasta topped with shrimp, asparagus, and some kind of tomato suace.

Cally fixed a taco for Mike, piling it with bean and meat filling, Cheddar cheese, guacamole, sour cream, ripe olives, lettuce, and tomatoes. Mike eyed it askance but gamely took a bite as Cally sampled the pasta he'd put on her plate. "Oh, this is heavenly," she murmured, sighing.

"Ziti con asparagi e scampi," Mike said. "My speciality, though I haven't cooked it in years."

Happy cleared his throat. "Not since that night you had the big fight with Marcia."

Cally glanced from one to the other. Mike seemed frozen, his fork in the air, a hard glitter to his eyes. Happy was staring down at his plate, toying with his food.

Mike swung his head to Cally, and the black look on his face sent a chill through her. "My former wife," he pronounced icily.

"And you're well rid of her," Happy added. He turned to Cally. "I don't know how Mike ever got involved with her anyway. I warned him."

"Let's drop the subject," Mike said. He didn't raise his voice even a fraction, but there was no question of his authority. Happy might berate Mike for anything he wanted, but Cally knew that when Mike drew the line Happy didn't cross it.

Mike turned the talk back to the food, but despite his efforts the rest of the meal fell flat. Cally kept darting her eyes back and forth between Happy and Mike. It hadn't occurred to her that Mike might have been married. Now she was curious about his ex-wife, but it was obvious that Mike hated discussing her.

They cleaned up the dishes in silence. Cally flipped on the switch for the light over the sink. There was a little pop and the light went out. Mike got the step stool and changed it for her, all without comment, and Cally noted to herself how much their mood had changed since before dinner. The Great American Drillers Cookoff had been a disaster.

Mike dried the last dish and hung the towel beside the stove. "I think I'll go on upstairs and lie down for a while," he said quietly. "Thanks for the lovely dinner, Cally. I'm sorry things didn't work out the way we'd planned."

She wanted to ask him about Marcia, but the wary expression in his eyes kept her silent. "I think I'll go read," she said.

She couldn't keep her mind on her book, and at ten she

turned out the kitchen light and went upstairs. There was a faint light under Mike's door, and Cally hesitated at her own room, then resolutely went in and shut the door. She had the feeling he was hurting from memories, and she ached for him because she knew what that was like. But she couldn't do anything for him unless he let her.

She finally dozed off but awoke later suddenly. She glanced at her bedside clock—two A.M. She lay in bed another minute, then got up and started for her door. Her hands were chapped and sore, and she wanted to get her hand lotion in the bathroom.

She padded into the hall barefoot, shivering. The night air was still chilly, and her sheer beige nightgown afforded no warmth.

She was feeling her way along the hall by instinct when she encountered something solid that shouldn't be there. She jumped, her mouth opening in a soundless gasp.

"Shhh," Mike whispered. "It's only your friendly neighborhood burglar." HIs hand touched her bare shoulder in a comforting gesture, and she stifled the urge to move into his arms. She wanted him to hold her tonight, because she was hurting, but she didn't know how to ask.

Her eyes adjusted to the lack of light and she could make out his dark hair and tall frame, wrapped in a robe.

"I couldn't sleep," he said. "I thought I'd go get a beer."

She nodded. His hand still rested on her bare shoulder. "You must be cold," he said suddenly, his eyes sweeping over the gown, lingering on the lacy cleft where the top of her breasts showed. He stepped closer to her and put his other arm around her, cradling her against him. She closed her eyes and let herself relax, burying her face in the matted hair of his chest where his robe opened.

"You're freezing," he said softly, his hands massaging her back. "You'd better get back in bed."

Hold me, she wanted to say. *Just for tonight, hold me and help me forget about Dan.* She opened her mouth as Mike held her away from him, and he watched her expectantly. "Well, good night," she said hesitantly.

"Good night, Cally." His hands stayed on her back as though he were loath to let go, and she wished he'd continue touching her like this. The blood was singing in her veins, and she no longer felt the night chill. She was almost trembling in her desire for him to hold her in an intimate embrace, but abruptly his hands withdrew, leaving her bereft.

"I'll see you tomorrow," he said hoarsely, and he hurried down the stairs. Cally closed her eyes to suppress a groan, pressing her fingertips against the lids. She told herself that the nights were always the hardest, but it seemed they were harder than ever now that Mike was in the same house.

Donna called Sunday morning to say she was going to be in the neighborhood and wanted to stop by that afternoon. "In the neighborhood?" Cally repeated skeptically. "Come on, Donna. The only thing in this neighborhood are cornfields. And don't tell me you're coming mushroom hunting. You buy all of yours in a gourmet shop."

"Ungrateful wretch," Donna sighed. "All right. I want to visit with you. Okay?"

Cally laughed. "Sure. I'll see you later."

Cally was alone when Donna's Trans Am pulled up to the house. The second driller had come up from St. Louis with the rig, and Mike and Happy had taken him over to George Fanning's drill site.

"So where is he?" Donna demanded as she stepped into the kitchen. "Do you lock him up in the closet on weekends?"

"Who are you talking about?" Cally asked innocently.

"*The* man," Donna said in exasperation. "The one who's living with you."

Donna lowered herself onto a kitchen chair, and Cally shook her head. "Not one man but two," Cally said. "I'm living a wild, uninhibited life. After I slop the hogs I run those two poor men ragged."

"Come on. Get serious. I want details here." Donna tapped one lacquered fingernail on the table.

"You lightened your hair again, didn't you?" Cally said, cocking her head.

Donna shook her head. "No, no. A perm and a frost job. Mr. René charges a fortune anymore, too. Now come on."

Cally sat down with a grin and pushed a can of diet soda toward Donna. "Okay," she said. "Happy and Mike are drillers. John hired them. They're staying here and two other drillers at John's."

"And what about the drive-in Friday night?"

"How did you find out about that?"

"Reba's sister does shampoos at Mr. René's."

"I don't know why I didn't just post a handbill," Cally said.

"Don't look so glum, honey. I think it's great that you're finally seeing someone. It's about time, you know. What's he like? Cute?"

"Cute hardly describes Mike Donovan," Cally said. "He's strong and gentle and tall and dark."

"Does he make your toes curl?"

"Uh-huh," Cally admitted, grinning in embarrassment.

"Then he's the one," Donna pronounced solemnly. "God, I'm happy for you, Cally."

"Don't go announcing our engagement or anything," Cally protested. "I've only known him a few days, and nothing serious has developed."

"It will," Donna assured her. "Just pretend you're not too interested. It gets them every time."

Donna was two years older, and Cally had watched in awe during high school as her cousin pampered and groomed a stable of contented boyfriends, trotting one or the other out when she wanted an escort. She had settled on Bill as her permanent steady with the same care she gave to choosing her prom gown, and deep down Cally suspected Bill had filled out a voluminous questionnaire and faced a battery of interviews before he was accorded the position as her future husband. In fact, Cally wouldn't be surprised if it was Donna who decided that Bill would be a lawyer.

Cally tried to imagine herself acting uninterested around Mike. She shook her head. "Mike's too sure of himself to be taken in by fake indifference."

"Then go the old honesty route and tell him you care about him. You do care about him, don't you?" She scrutinized Cally over her diet soda.

"You make getting a man sound like assembling a bike."

"Twice as easy," Donna said with a little shake of her head. "You didn't answer me. Do you want this man?"

Cally gave a little shrug. "He makes me feel like no one ever has . . ." She trailed off, lowering her eyes in embarrassment.

Donna reached over and patted her arm. "Honey, you deserve a little magic in your life, and it sounds like you've found it. I'd like to meet this Mike Donovan. If that dreamy haze in your eyes is any indication he's a man well worth meeting."

"He's interesting," Cally allowed.

"Well, it looks like I'm not going to pry any more information out of you, so I might as well tell you why I'm really here. I've got a man interested in your farm."

Cally felt her heart constrict. "A buyer?"

"Now don't get that look on your face, honey. Just be open about this. He's married with three children. I showed him a picture of the farm, and he fell in love with it. Cally, he and his wife are really excited about fixing it up." Her eyes searched Cally's face. "You're wasting away here trying to keep up with everything by yourself. It's no good, Cally."

"I can't sell the farm," Cally protested, tensing her shoulders.

"This may sound brutal, but here it is anyway. Nowhere is it engraved in stone that you can't sell this farm. Dan was selfish to insist you two live here anyway. He should've known it would never amount to anything. You had to quit your job just to feed his farmer fantasy."

"Please, Donna." Cally shut her eyes painfully.

"All right," Donna said in a softer voice. "I'm sorry. But it's the truth." She glanced at her watch. "Listen, I've got to run. There's a luncheon at the country club today." She stood up and pointed a lacquered fingernail at Cally. "You take my advice and think about selling. I know you've turned down every other buyer I've gotten for you, but think about this one. And don't let Mike Donovan get away from you either."

"Yes, Mother," Cally said lightly.

"I'm serious. He sounds too good to let go."

Cally stood at the door watching the Trans Am back out of the drive, visions of herself tracking down Mike Donovan like a wild animal chasing through her head. Maybe she should set one of those rope snares that would tighten when he stepped on it, then hoist him upside down in the air. Picturing Donovan dangling from the redbud tree made her smile. But her humor faded when she also pictured a FOR SALE sign on the lawn.

Chapter Five

"YOU CAN'T STAY for the 4-H meeting, Mike," Cally repeated for the tenth time.

"What if I put on a skirt and stick a ribbon in my hair?" His voice was innocently coaxing, and she summoned all of her resistance.

"That's tempting, but no. Not even if you brought a handmade pincushion. The girls just wouldn't be comfortable. Besides, Laura Colman is giving a demonstration on baking brownies tonight, and she's very shy. It's taken me almost a year to build up her confidence enough for her to stand in front of the club."

"Baking brownies? I didn't know you 4-H'ers were at war with the Girl Scouts. How did you capture a Brownie anyway?"

"Not a Girl Scout Brownie," she said acidly, planting her hands on her hips to lend added weight to her refusal.

Mike sighed, then apparently decided to try another tack. Adopting a look of wounded pride, he said, "Aren't you even going to save me a brownie?"

Cally pursed her lips, amused by his eagerness to stay for the meeting. "You know how hungry eight-year-old girls are. I'll be lucky if they don't clean out my refrigerator."

"Then I definitely have to stay and protect my valuables.

Part of that food in the refrigerator is mine."

"Donovan," she said in her best take-charge voice.

He held up his hand in defeat. "Say no more. I'll leave.
I guess I could go play cards with Happy and the boys at
the Masterses'."

He looked so morose that Cally had to smile. She es-
corted him to the door, then drew back in horror. "Oh no."

"What is it?" he demanded.

"That's Laura coming up the drive. And her mother's
with her. That's like having a wolf escort the lamb. That
woman makes poor little Laura so nervous I know she'll
never get through her demonstration."

"Don't worry. Let me stay, and I'll keep Laura's mother
occupied."

She hesitated just long enough to gauge the determination
on Mrs. Colman's face. "Thanks, Mike," she murmured.
Cally opened the kitchen door and glanced from mother to
daughter. "Hello, Laura, Mrs. Colman. Come on in." Uh-
oh. Mrs. Colman looked like a naval officer about to begin
inspection. Cally glanced at Mike, and he raised his eyebrows with a soundless whistle.

Mrs. Colman pulled off her leather gloves and patted her
curly brown hair. Cally had learned from the other mothers
that Mrs. Colman had Laura when she was almost forty,
and she'd been divorced shortly after. No doubt that ac-
counted for some of her overprotectiveness of the child.

"I'll help Laura get ready for her demonstration," Mrs.
Colman announced. "Take off your coat, Laura." Laura
looked absolutely miserable.

"Mrs. Colman," Mike said smoothly, intervening with
a smile. "I'm a friend of Cally's—Mike Donovan. Maybe
you can help me. Cally asked me to help set up the chairs,
and I don't know where to begin. Would you mind terribly?"
Cally watched Mike's pitch with fascinated detachment. He
was definitely skilled at dealing with people. His face and
voice conveyed just the right amount of male helplessness,
and Cally could tell that Mrs. Colman was charmed.

"Don't forget the flags," Cally reminded him, and Mike
turned, his arm around Mrs. Colman's shoulders, and
winked.

Cally set about helping Laura organize her demonstration

equipment on the kitchen table, and soon the other girls started arriving.

Mike had set up the folding chairs in three rows of four each, talking to Mrs. Colman the whole time, and then he'd made a show of asking her advice on how to set up the two flags, one American, one 4-H. Now he had her engaged in conversation in the last row, and Cally saw that Laura was visibly more relaxed. And Mrs. Colman was paying rapt attention to Mike.

The meeting got under way as a little girl tapped her gavel importantly on the kitchen table and another little girl read the minutes, stumbling over a couple of words, but obviously pleased with her office.

The business portion of the meeting finished, Cally glanced at Laura with an encouraging smile and saw the little girl swallow nervously. Mrs. Colman had come to attention at the back of the kitchen. "Laura has a lovely demonstration for us tonight," Cally said. "She's going to make brownies. Laura, go ahead and just relax. Be yourself."

Cally sat back down in the front row, trying to give Laura moral support with her eyes. She found herself on the edge of her seat, her hands knotted in her lap as Laura began to speak in a trembling voice.

Laura's hands were shaking as she turned on the electric mixer to whip the eggs in the bowl, and Cally's knuckles were white. "Then you put in two cups of sugar," Laura almost whispered, her eyes glued to the bowl. She turned on the mixer again and swallowed hard. "Then you add half a cup of melted butter and . . ." Her tiny voice was receding into nothingness, and Cally strained forward on her chair. The little girl's eyes darted frantically around the room, and Cally smiled and nodded, trying to encourage her. Her cherubic face was paling, and Cally knew stage fright was overcoming her. She stammered something almost inaudible about the butter again, and her lower lip began to tremble. The other girls were beginning to titter.

Cally was about to stand up and tell her she didn't have to finish when Mike's voice boomed from behind. "I love brownies. I'd sure like to know how to make them."

The room had suddenly gone so quiet that a pin could

have been heard dropping as Mike made his way to the kitchen table. "Do you really know how to make brownies?" he asked seriously, sitting down at the table so that he was level with her. Well, almost. She still had to look up slightly.

Laura nodded, her nervousness forgotten in the face of Mike's interruption.

"What do you do with this flour?" Mike demanded. "Do you pour it on top?"

"No, silly." Laura giggled. "First you have to put the chocolate in. Like this." Forgetting about her audience, she put the chocolate and butter in the bowl and stirred it. "Then the flour," she said importantly, stirring that in.

"What about these nuts?" Mike asked. "Do we get to eat these?" He pretended to pop one into his mouth, and Laura laughed. "Don't you know anything about cooking? They go in the brownies."

All the little girls giggled as an exaggerated look of disappointment crept over Mike's face.

"Then we bake them," Laura pronounced.

"When do we eat them?" Mike asked.

"I brought some already baked," Laura said, beaming as she removed the aluminum foil from another pan.

Mike reached in and popped one of the brownies into his mouth. "Delicious!" he cried, rolling his eyes to everyone's laughter. "This little lady is a real cook." He leaped to his feet and led the applause for Laura's demonstration while she glowed, her eyes shining.

Cally stood up to serve the refreshments and leaned close to Mike as she passed. "Way to go, champ."

He grinned back at her and whispered, "I'll collect my thanks later."

The girls were all happily munching cookies and brownies and drinking Kool-Aid, and Mrs. Colman was asking Mike's advice about her birch tree, which was suffering from some fungus, when Laura came up to Cally, her mouth ringed with a purple Kool-Aid stain. Solemnly, she said, "Mrs. Taylor, I want to do my demonstration at the county fair."

"That's wonderful, Laura," Cally exclaimed, genuinely happy with the girl's newfound confidence.

"And I want to take him with me," Laura said, pointing at Mike.

"We'll see," Cally said, patting Laura's shoulder. "We'll have to check Mr. Donovan's schedule."

Once the meeting ended Mike acted as official doorman, escorting each giggling girl to her car. After the last little girl had been picked up by her mother and the last car had pulled away, he came back inside.

Cally dried a plate and turned to watch him. She leaned back against the sink, twirling the dish towel in one hand. "You were the hit of the evening," she observed.

Mike sank down at the table and propped his feet on a nearby chair. "Laura was the real heroine. She turned out to be quite the cook, didn't she?"

Cally nodded and stared down at the floor. "You put on quite a performance yourself."

"I enjoyed coming to Laura's rescue."

"And entertaining Mrs. Colman?"

She glanced at him and saw that his face had become wary. He frowned slightly. "What's this about, Cally? Surely you're not jealous of Mrs. Colman."

Cally shook her head quickly. "It troubles me, Mike," she began hesitantly. "I watched you tonight. You handled the girls and Laura's mother so well. You had them all mesmerized. You charm people very easily."

"Somehow I don't think you meant that as a compliment." His eyes had gone flinty, and a sharp edge crept into his voice. He crossed his arms over his chest and inclined his head slightly, his expression almost challenging her to continue.

Cally's gaze wavered, and she carefully hung up the dish towel before she took a seat opposite him. Despite his relaxed pose she sensed the coiled tension in him.

She picked her words carefully. "It just seems very easy for you to get people to do what you want."

"I think what you're trying to say is that I manipulate people." Incisive as always, he'd cut through her delicate phrasing.

"All right. That's what occurred to me as I watched you tonight. I began to wonder how much is an act."

He slowly lowered his feet from the chair and leaned forward on the table. "And you're wondering how much of the time I'm pretending with you."

She was afraid to look at him, having had her doubt finally put into words, and when she did she held her breath. Hard and glittering, his eyes were like chipped ice. The angles of his face seemed sharper. The heat from the cooling oven filled the kitchen, but it wasn't a comforting warmth she felt. It was the crackling heat of tension. She laced and unlaced her hands on the table.

Mike's hand resounded as he hit the table with his open palm, and Cally jumped as though a shot had gone off. "Dammit, Cally, I don't pretend with you. Don't you know that?" He stood up abruptly and paced the floor, raking a hand through his hair. He stopped and came back to the table. He leaned forward, resting his open hands on the table, and faced her squarely. "I can help a little girl forget her nervousness, and maybe I can distract a meddling mother, but I don't manipulate. And I especially don't manipulate you, Cally. I've never hidden anything from you or pretended to be anything I'm not."

Cally took a deep breath. "What about Marcia?"

His eyes narrowed and he lowered his head. "Cally," he said softly. Slowly he sat down, lifting his hands in a helpless gesture. "Even Happy doesn't know everything about that."

"And I don't know anything," Cally protested.

"Is it important to you?" Something in his voice warned her that she was asking a lot of him at this moment, and suddenly she wasn't sure what right she had to ask.

"No," she said carefully. "It's not important."

He watched her as she stood up and took off her apron, laying it on the back of the chair. "I'll tell you whatever you want to know," he said softly, but still there was an edge to his voice.

She was sorry now that she'd brought it up, sorry that she'd intruded into his past like this. She was assuming there was something intimate between them by asking him about his former wife. "I don't want to know, Mike," she said decisively. "I'm sorry I said what I did. Good night."

"Good night, Cally."

She stopped at the stairs and looked back into the kitchen. He was sitting at the table, his back to her and his hands on the table. From the set of his shoulders, Cally surmised that he was still agitated.

At the moment, she hated the suspicions that had festered in her tonight as she'd watched him deal so charmingly with Laura and her mother. She had picked at that as though she were desperate to find some fault with him. Was she programmed to self-destruct or what? The man was good with people, and she attacked him as if it were one of the Seven Deadly Sins. Way to go, Cally.

The next few days were tense, and Cally sensed that Mike had his guard up whenever they were alone. Fortunately, they weren't thrown together too much. She spent her days struggling with the Bucyrus Erie while he drilled on John's site. He usually came in late for dinner and retired early. When his eyes met hers over the table they were flat and expressionless.

By the fourth day she was ready to scream from sheer frustration.

She threw her nervous energy into sewing in the evening. She'd bought a dotted Swiss fabric several years ago to make new bedroom curtains, but she'd never finished the project.

By Saturday she had the two sets of curtains done, and she carried the step stool up to her room after lunch to hang them. Happy had gone with the two boys in the pickup to bring back fresh water for mixing the concrete to set casing, and Mike was downstairs reading the St. Louis newspaper he'd picked up at the pharmacy that morning.

Cally dumped her sweater drawer with its keepsakes onto the bed and rooted until she found a screwdriver to tighten the hooks. She slipped the curtains onto the rod, then balanced precariously on the step stool as she hung the rod. With infinite care she tied back the curtains with the strips she'd made from the same material. Gently she fingered her handiwork. She should have taken down the venetian blinds ages ago. The room was much lighter and more airy now. Dappled sunlight fell on the wooden floor, spilling over onto the braided rug that contained so many pieces of her grandmother's old dresses. When she'd spent nights at her grandmother's house as a little girl, she'd curled up on the couch in front of the fireplace and watched in fascination as her grandmother pieced together the rugs from scraps. Looking at them now brought back the warmth she'd enjoyed.

Sighing, she ran her finger over the glass pane. The windows needed washing. They looked especially grimy with the new curtains up.

"You did a nice job."

She spun around, nearly toppling off the step stool, and he reached up his arms, putting a hand on either side of her waist to steady her.

"I didn't hear you come in," she said, tingling warmth spreading up from his hands. His fingers began a soft massage, and her knees felt suddenly shaky. She rested her hands on his shoulders and experienced a jolt, as if she'd just made an electrical connection. Gently he lifted her down, his hands lingering on her waist before he stepped back with a wry smile. She saw the spark in his eyes, and it made her heart leap.

"Here, let me hang the other one for you."

She threaded the curtains onto the second rod and handed it to him, standing back to watch as he carefully settled it on the hooks.

"There," he said, stepping down from the stool and admiring the window. "That makes a world of difference."

"It was rather depressing with those old blinds."

Mike looked around the room with a satisfied smile, then sat down on the bed, pushing aside two cardigans. He picked up her high school yearbook and began leafing through it. Cally tied back the curtains Mike had hung and folded the step stool, leaning it against the wall. She began putting sweaters back in the drawer, watching Mike from the corner of her eye. She saw him stop at her senior picture and smile. Cally grimaced and turned back to the drawer, her hands automatically folding and refolding a sweater. She'd worn a pixie cut in high school, and under her picture it said her ambition was to own her own restaurant and have six kids.

She dared a glance back at Mike and found him grinning at her devilishly. "Sparky?" he said in amusement.

Her nickname in school. She'd forgotten about that. She shrugged lamely. "We built a high-voltage coil in physics class. You know, where the electric spark jumps from one prong to another." Mike nodded. "My lab partner, Harley— the one from the car dealership..." She gave Mike a reproachful look. "Anyway, Harley took my English composition and stuck it between the prongs and burned little holes all over it. I got my nickname after I tried to explain to Mrs. Fiedler what happened."

He glanced back at the page. "A restaurant and six kids. Well, I could help you with the kids. The restaurant I'm not so sure about."

Cally felt heat flood her face, and she picked up another sweater and picked imaginary lint off it. "I've changed some since then."

"Seven kids, eight—you name it," Mike said, his tone seemingly innocuous, but his expression suggestive. His lips twitched slightly. "We could even buy the kids a family pet and all of us could go for Sunday walks. Two boys and two girls would be nice for a start. The dog could be either."

"Mike," she began with a helpless gesture.

"Don't you think you ought to put that sweater down now?" he asked gently. "It's going to be bald if you keep picking at it like that."

She smiled weakly and folded the sweater one more time. Reluctantly she dropped it in the drawer and stood staring down at it. Her 4-H ribbons and high school awards were in that drawer, too. All neatly ordered, like her sweaters. And then Mike had to come into her life like a March wind intent on blowing everything into disarray.

"Daniel Taylor," Mike said quietly, and Cally jumped. He was looking at the yearbook, and she saw Dan's picture—blond, solemn. "Inseparable from Cally," Mike read. "Likes basketball, student council, and farming. President of the F.F.A."

"Future Farmers of America," Cally said dully.

"Well, he was indeed a future farmer," Mike said with a humorless smile as he closed the yearbook.

"Dan was a nice guy," she said fiercely. She could feel tears pricking the backs of her eyes.

"I didn't say he wasn't," Mike said softly. "I'm only

trying to understand you, Cally, and it seems I'll have to understand Dan before I can do that."

"He worked hard, and he was trying to build something for the future," she said defensively. Despite her efforts, the tears were beginning to trickle down her cheek.

She mopped her face with the back of her hand, and Mike seemed to materialize suddenly at her side, pulling her into his arms. "Let it out, Cally," he whispered soothingly. She turned her face to his shoulder, overcome with great, wracking sobs. Her pain was so real at that moment that it might have been an open cut on her heart.

Gently, Mike led her to the bed and sat down, keeping her close against him. He was murmuring soothing words of comfort, stroking her hair. Slowly her sobs died to hiccupping sniffles.

"I'm sorry," she said, choking on the words. "I don't usually lose control like that.".

"And that's your problem," he admonished her. "You can't keep it bottled up inside you."

She didn't know how long they sat like that, Mike rocking her as the afternoon drew on, but the sun's rays had withdrawn from the braided rug when she lifted her head. She was looking straight into his eyes, and her breath caught as his eyes burned back into hers, as though trying to cauterize her pain.

His lips brushed each eyelid, kissing the wet lashes with a tenderness that made her tremble. His hand clasped her neck, his thumb sensuously massaging her earlobe. She wasn't sure when comfort became arousal, but her blood began to whirl in heated excitement. His mouth found its way to her own, and she met it eagerly, her hands clutching at his hair, reveling in the coarse texture as it flowed between her fingers.

As long as he touched her, the ache inside was gone, and she strained to keep him close. He began to unbutton her blouse, and her hands fluttered restlessly on his chest, her gaze focused on his face, concentrating on the fire in his eyes.

He lowered her onto her back, reached behind her and unfastened her bra and slowly opened her blouse. Cally gasped as his hand closed gently over her breast, kneading it as his thumb teased the nipple into hard awareness. He planted slow, arousing kisses on her throat before his lips moved lower to circle her breast. "You're beautiful," he whispered, and his warm breath sent tremors through her. Slowly his lips took possession of the nipple, and his tongue tasted with an exquisite pressure that arched her back. The room whirled away from her mind, leaving only Mike and the resurrection of her body.

Her mouth half-opened in protest as he drew away, his hands lingering on her naked flesh. She fastened her gaze on his dexterous fingers as he began unbuttoning his shirt, her skin still tingling from the magic those fingers had worked.

A cloud must have passed over the sun, because the ray of light on the floor died out suddenly, and Cally felt a shadow lengthening over the room. With a fierceness that nearly made her gasp out loud, overwhelming guilt tore through her. The ache Mike had kept at bay claimed her with renewed force, freezing passion with icy strength. She held her fist to her mouth and tried to focus on Mike's face, but she couldn't escape it.

He'd thrown his shirt on the floor and was lowering himself to her, his chest strong and firm, lightly matted with dark hair. He was offering himself to her, she thought in distraction, and she couldn't receive his gift.

Unable to speak for a moment, she slowly shook her head, her eyes filling with tears again. "I can't, Mike," she whispered. "Not here, not now."

His face clouded, and something filled his eyes. It was more than disappointment but not anger. She almost would have said it was grief. "All right, honey," he whispered raggedly, gently. "It's all right." He cradled her to him and rocked her gently before he began fastening the buttons on her blouse.

"I'm sorry," she said. "I just can't seem to stop thinking about Dan. This was our room."

She knew she'd said the wrong thing when he withdrew his fingers abruptly. He picked up his shirt and shrugged into it, avoiding her eyes. "He's dead, Cally," he said quietly, looking at her as he fastened the buttons. "You can't let your happiness die with him."

She shrugged tensely. "It isn't that. I just don't feel right about you and me here in this room."

"It's your room." His voice was sharp, and she flushed angrily.

"I'm trying to explain," she retorted, her fingers fumbling with her hair.

"You've already explained," Mike said.

"No, I haven't. Because you won't listen." She stood up in agitated anger. "Dan was a part of my life."

Mike turned and started to leave the room while Cally clenched her hands at her sides. He stopped suddenly at her closet door, which stood partially open. With one violent jerk of his hand he flung the door wide, revealing Dan's shirts and jeans still hung neatly beside Cally's dresses.

With a soft groan she sank down onto the bed, her hands clutching at the chenille spread.

"He's still a part of your life," Mike said with acid coldness. He swung on his heel, then stood motionless a moment before turning back to her. His face was hard and stark with the intensity of his anger. His eyes left hers briefly as he glanced at the window. "Maybe you should take the curtains back down, Cally. They bring too much life to this room."

Chapter Six

CALLY WENT THROUGH the motions of feeding and watering the livestock that evening as the sun set, but she did everything by rote. Her mind was back in her bedroom with Mike. She was still arguing with him, still experiencing that numbing shock when he accused her of living in the past with Dan.

The worst part was that she couldn't tell Mike that she hurt inside because she felt things with him that she'd never felt with Dan. And that was eating her up. Every time Mike touched her and passion ripped through her body like an explosion, she felt she was betraying Dan's memory. What right did she have to feel such incredible pleasure when he was dead?

She leaned on the wooden fence by the hog lot, watching the sow with her latest litter, all of them lounging in the mud like pink Jell-O on a brown plate. She rested her booted foot on one rail and leaned forward on her forearms. She heard the kitchen screen door slam, and automatically she stiffened. She and Mike had walked a tenuous line around each other the rest of the afternoon, and when she walked into the kitchen he quickly left, avoiding her eyes.

The footsteps approaching her were heavier than Mike's and slower.

"You okay?"

"Sure, Happy," she said, giving him a quick smile over her shoulder. He looked uncomfortable as he dug one toe into the soft earth. She turned back to the hogs, thinking that Happy's thinning hair looked as though he'd taken care to slick it down over his bald spot before he came to talk to her.

"I guess you and Mike had a fight." She could hear the embarrassed concern in his voice.

"A slight misunderstanding." Her voice was faint, and she scrutinized the hogs as though she were judging a contest.

Happy cleared his throat. "From the way Mike's grumping around it seems like a bit of a big misunderstanding to me."

"Did he send you out here?"

Happy snorted. "Lord, no! He'd throw a fit if he knew I was talking to you about it. He's not one to let others inside his troubles."

"Apparently he confided in you about his troubles with Marcia," she pointed out. She turned around and rested her hands on the top railing behind her.

Happy shook his head. "Mike never told nobody about what happened between him and Marcia." He shrugged. "All I knew was they was fighting a lot. I never liked her much anyway." With that offhand dismissal he looked over his shoulder at the house. "I better get back in. You want me to fix you a sandwich for dinner?"

"No, thanks, Happy. I'll be in in a few minutes."

She watched him amble back to the house, his bowlegged gait stiff and slow. She stood for a while after he'd disappeared inside, staring up at the sky. Fleecy white clouds collected on the horizon, soaking in the purple and pink hues of the dying sun, sopping it up like cotton balls absorbing watercolor. The hogs were restless, banging the metal feeders, snorting at each other in irritation.

The damp chill of impending dusk was settling around her, so she slowly pushed away from the fence and walked back to the house. She walked toward the sink to wash up. The kitchen was deserted, but the aroma of cooking beef hung in the air. She dried her hands, got a can of soda from the refrigerator, and walked to the table. She started to raise the can to her lips and stopped in mid-motion. There was a plate at her place and on it was a hamburger, the top half of the bun lying next to the burger, lettuce and tomato neatly arranged beside that. What arrested her attention was the hamburger itself. On it was a message. Really it was mustard, but it had been squeezed on top the way someone would write Happy Birthday on a cake. But this message read, *I'm sorry.* True, it was a little sloppy. There must have been some air bubbles in the plastic container of mustard. But it was innovative. She had to give him that. Slowly she shook her head from side to side and sank down on the chair.

Instinctively she glanced up and saw him standing in the doorway. "I figured I'd probably worn out the white flag bit," he said with a crooked smile. "You'd never go for that again."

She shook her head again. He sighed. "And since the only florists are in Quincy, I was afraid it might take three days to get delivery out here. And I didn't want you to stay mad at me for three days."

"You are certifiably insane." All she could do was look at him helplessly, feeling her heart pound with unaccountable fervor at the sight of him standing there so indolently.

He raised his eyebrows and looked at her with the hopefulness of a schoolboy who had just presented the teacher with a homemade valentine. "It wasn't easy trying to write with one of those fat mustard barrels," he said.

"Cramped your fingers, did it?"

"Do you know, Cally Taylor, that you're not an easy woman to apologize to?"

"You shouldn't end a sentence with a preposition." She crossed her arms and leaned back.

"And you shouldn't make sport of the man who cooked you a hamburger." A devilish gleam stole into his eyes, and he pushed himself away from the doorframe. "If it's grammar you want to discuss, then we'll talk about grammar."

"Is there going to be a test on this?" Cally demanded, feeling the first stirrings of her heated pulse as Mike slowly walked toward her.

"You bet there is," he growled, taking her hand and

pulling her to her feet. "Let's discuss nouns first. Now, do you suppose you could think of a word that's a noun?"

"Hamburger?" she suggested with owlish innocence.

Mike shook his head. "You're hopeless." With coaxing hands he drew her into his arms. "A kiss," he whispered against her ear. "Now that's a noun worth remembering."

"I think you're going to have to show me," she said, her heart singing. "I'm a slow learner."

He nudged her earlobe softly with his lips, tasting and teasing a trail to her mouth by way of her jawline. She anticipated a light, exploratory touch, but his mouth devoured hers in a gesture of insatiable hunger. He caught her lower lip in his teeth and gently worried it, making the sensitive area tingle with sharp jolts of electricity. His tongue touched where his teeth had been and further explored the inner recesses of her mouth. Sparks seemed to go off in her head as his mouth pressed hers in intimate communion.

Gradually the pressure of his lips lessened, brushing hers lightly. He drew back until his head was a few inches from hers. "That, my lady, is a kiss," he whispered, and she could see his pulse hammering at the base of his throat.

"Yes, it certainly is." She expelled her breath slowly, wanting to hold the taste of him as long as she could. "Do I pass nouns?"

"With flying colors." His eyes moved over her face with riveting intensity. "Want to move on to verbs?"

She nodded mutely, giving him a dreamy smile.

"To adore," he murmured.

She swallowed, giddy with the tension of wanting him. His touch was as enticing and heady as a glass of champagne—light, alive, and intoxicating. The golden flecks in his eyes seemed to draw her into him like irresistible magnets. She pressed herself to his body as the world melted away. It was a journey to the heart, and she felt a throb of life that matched the cadence of his pulse. It was as though the boundaries of skin and bone ceased to exist as she traveled to the wellspring where desire and life itself began. She could read his passion and tenderness in each minute twitch of muscle. His sinew and bone became hers, and her eyes went smoky with possessive greed.

His lips parted on the slender column of her neck, nibbling the throbbing cord there. His breath feathered shivers through each nerve ending as he alternately kissed her neck and gave it light nips with his teeth. His fingers slid over her collarbone, caressing the hollows and curves of her shoulders. She kissed him in return when he raised his head, tasting the curve of his jaw, tangy, and the musky hollow at the base of his throat. He dipped his hands in her hair, letting it flow over his palms like liquid silk. She felt his breath against her hair as he whispered her name softly.

Happy's voice reached them from the stairs. "Has Cally come back in yet?" He cleared his throat noisily as he entered the kitchen and abruptly halted. "Oh, uh, sorry," he said, coughing. "I didn't know you two were here." He rocked back on his heels and scratched the bald spot on his head. "Well now, I guess I'll go on up to bed. Uh, good night." He was slowly backing out of the kitchen. Mike's arms were still locked around her, and Cally slowly came back to earth. For the last few minutes, the room had ceased to be her kitchen in all its ordinariness. It had become an extraordinary haven where her senses took flight.

"Cally and I were just going over some English grammar," Mike said lightly, his fingers still stroking the back of her neck.

Happy looked from one to the other and sighed. "Well, carry on," he began. "What I mean is . . ." he said, embarrassed.

"Never mind," Mike laughed.

Happy retreated, mumbling to himself as he climbed the stairs.

Mike turned back to Cally and in a husky voice asked, "Want to try adjectives?"

"Mmmmm." She buried her head against his throat again. "Let's start with magnificent." His husky laughter vibrated against her ear. "I think you're ready for graduate work, lady."

It was late when she made her way—regretfully—upstairs.

Mike was already making coffee when she came into the kitchen the next morning, and she looked at the clock in surprise. "What are you doing up so early?" she asked.

"That sounds almost insulting," he said cheerfully, pouring her a cup. "Most days I make it out of bed by noon."

"What's the occasion?" she asked suspiciously.

"All right." He threw up his hands in mock despair. "I have an ulterior motive." He sat down at the table and gave her an enthusiastic smile. "I thought we'd have a picnic today, and I wanted to make the arrangements this morning."

"A picnic?" She shrugged. "Why not wait until the weekend? Don't you have to drill today?"

"Happy and the boys can get along without me for a couple of hours this afternoon," he said evasively.

"There's something you're not telling me about this. Is this some kind of secret picnic or what?"

"I've got to go back to St. Louis for a while," he said, watching her face. "We've got a new job there."

"What about John's well?" She could feel a cold dread growing with each passing second. It hadn't occurred to her that he might have to leave before the wells had been completed.

"John's in no rush," Mike said, steepling his fingers under his chin, elbows on the table. "He told me to go ahead and accept the new job, then get up here when I can. He and his wife are enjoying the boys' company, so they're going to continue to stay there while Happy and I are in St. Louis."

"When are you leaving?" She wished she hadn't asked it as soon as she saw his eyes darken. If the sun had disappeared at that moment she couldn't have felt more abandoned.

"Tomorrow morning. I'm sorry, Cally."

Her eyes swung to the mantel clock. The glass face bore a faded hand-painted picture of a flock of wild geese flying in front of a full moon. A corner of the glass was chipped where she'd hit it with one of her grandfather's darts when she was five. She'd started crying when she'd told her grandmother about it, but she had held Cally and told her it didn't matter.

Cally felt like she'd broken the glass all over again, powerless to assuage the ache in her heart.

"Maybe now I can get some drilling done myself," she

said brightly, turning to him with a forced smile. "You've kept me pretty well occupied." She stood up and walked to the stove to pour herself another cup of coffee. "Actually I ought to set some casing today. Maybe we can make the picnic another time."

"Don't, Cally. You don't have any casing to set."

She took a deep breath and turned from the stove. "Don't what?"

"Don't pretend it doesn't matter. That it's not important."

"And how should I react?" she demanded. "You're taking off tomorrow. I don't seem to have much control over that."

"We still have today. Let's have the picnic."

"Sure," she said blithely. "One last fling." She hadn't meant it to sound that sarcastic, and she was sorry the instant she saw his jaw muscle tighten.

"Fine," Mike said sharply, standing up. "I'll go pick up some chicken at lunchtime and meet you here." He slammed his coffee cup down on the counter and stalked toward the door. "I'm sure we'll have a wonderful time," he said blackly, banging the screen door on his way out.

"I'm sure," Cally muttered. Despite the fact that she'd succeeded in making him angry, she felt worse than ever. If she'd intended to make him feel bad about leaving, her guilty conscience wouldn't let her enjoy her victory. And worse yet, she might have ruined their last chance to be alone together.

She couldn't work up any enthusiasm to drill, so she dug in the flower bed all morning, sprinkling marigold and petunia seeds on the freshly troweled earth by the east side of the house, where morning sun would reach them. It would be nice if human beings were as predictable as flowers, she thought grumpily. A little water, a little sun, a touch of fertilizer, and flowers brought forth all kinds of delightful color. There was no pleasing some humans. But then, flowers shriveled and died if there was too much water or too much sun, whereas humans seemed far hardier, at least on the surface.

You're waxing philosophical, Cally. A sure sign you're in trouble. Why not act like a mature adult and talk things out with Mike?

"I can do without the voice of reason," she muttered out

loud. "I don't want to talk things out with him."

Mature, Cally, really mature.

"Oh, shut up," Cally muttered. "If you think you can handle Mike Donovan any better, you're welcome to try." She glanced around furtively and stood up, shaking her head. She was actually arguing out loud with herself. Her hold on sanity was more tenuous than she'd thought.

As promised, Mike appeared at noon, bearing a cardboard bucket of fried chicken and biscuits from Gordon's Grill. Cally had filled a paper sack with some apples, brownies, and carrot sticks. She carefully put it between them on Bunky's seat.

"I asked Gordon if he had a little Chardonnay to go with this," Mike said dryly, "but he said he didn't mess with those funny vegetables."

"You could have substituted his lemonade," Cally said, her eyes on the worn path he was taking between the pasture and the cornfield. "He never cleans the machine, and the stuff's all fermented."

They rode in silence, bouncing over the ruts, and Cally refrained from asking where they were headed. If he'd solicited her advice she would have suggested a spot near the pond. The first year she and Dan were married she used to go ice skating there alone in the winter—Dan claimed he didn't have the time—but now the pond was nearly dry because of the burrowing muskrats. Mike wasn't driving toward the pond though. He pulled up beside a spreading hazelnut tree and stopped.

"How did you find this place?" Cally asked, swallowing.

"I took a long walk yesterday." He frowned as he faced her. "Why? Don't you like it?"

"Actually it's one of my favorite spots," she said quietly, opening the door. "I come here a lot." She came in the summer with a book when she wanted to escape the house, or in the fall when the hazelnuts were ripe. The squirrels generally beat her to the crop, but often she found enough for Christmas cookies. She showed Dan this place one day— her special place—and pulled his head down to hers and kissed him. . . . But that was Dan and that was a long time ago.

She and Mike spread a blanket on the ground where a

grassy slope began to curve down to the bank of the stream just beyond the tree. It was a perfectly shaded glade, nestled among cedar trees that stood guard at the edge of the bank where soft red earth was studded with limestone rock and white-blossomed wild strawberries.

Cally sat down on the blanket and leaned over to touch a clump of violets on the bank. Deep purple flowers with white faces, they looked like cool, intricately carved chips of amethyst. She brushed her fingers over one of the heart-shaped leaves and abruptly pulled back.

"I even provided a floral centerpiece," Mike said, nodding toward the violets. "Candlelight I don't have, unless you want me to get the flashlight from the truck."

"This is fine," Cally said quietly.

Mike tightened his lips and tilted back his head. "Maybe you were right. Maybe it isn't a good time for a picnic."

Cally's eyes flew to his face. "I didn't mean to be so out-of-sorts this morning," she said slowly. "I guess I was pretty . . . well . . ."

"Crabby?" Mike suggested. "Unreasonable? Totally infuriating?"

"All of the above," she said with a wry smile. "Listen, I'm sorry."

"It's all right." He reached across the blanket and cupped her face in his hand. "I was a little edgy myself."

She always seemed to be apologizing to him. Living alone certainly hadn't improved her ability to sustain a relationship.

His shoulder brushed hers as he leaned closer, and he kissed her with a gentleness made all the more tender by their surroundings. Carefully he released her chin but continued to hold her mouth captive as he pulled her over so that she was lying on her back in his lap. His leg was bent, supporting her back.

Her hair spread over his leg in a silky curtain, and he carefully brushed it back from her face as though lifting a veil.

"You look troubled," he whispered, his mouth seeking the sensitive hollow at the base of her throat, eliciting a husky groan from deep inside her. Clouds of doubt hung in the back of her mind, but Mike's touch effectively obliterated coherent thought. "Don't think about anything. Just let me love you." His voice was hypnotic, and she found her hand straying to his chest, toying with his shirt buttons.

"Yes, honey," he whispered. "Touch me." His lips were sending tremors over the flesh were the V of her pink pullover sweater ended. He tugged up the sweater and groaned appreciatively. She hadn't worn a bra today, and her breasts tightened as the cool air caressed them. His mouth lowered to take her nipple between his teeth. Her head dipped back over his knee, and her hands clutched at his shirt. The rhythm of her fingers as she stroked his chest matched the rhythm of his mouth, and her own mouth opened soundlessly.

He was unfastening her jeans, and she ground her eyes tightly shut as Dan's face swam before her. *No*, she protested fiercely, *she wouldn't think of that now*. But it was futile. As Mike slid his hands inside her jeans she gasped sharply, and her eyes flew open, spilling over with guilt and grief.

Mike read her expression, and immediately his hands stilled. Slowly he raised his head. *Don't look at me that way*, she wanted to say. *Don't make me ache any more than I do already*.

"It's Dan, isn't it?" he demanded, a razor edge to his voice. When she didn't answer, just stared at him miserably, he leaned his head back and sighed raggedly. When those blue eyes swung back to her they were sapphire daggers. "Are these his trees, Cally? Is this his stream? Is there any place here where his ghost doesn't exist?"

"You don't understand," she said miserably, sitting up and pulling her sweater back down. "He was here with me once."

"Keep your memories," he said through clenched teeth. "But don't relive them with me, Cally. He's not here now."

She stared at him helplessly, her frustration and pain growing. No, it wasn't what he thought. When she had drawn Dan into her arms and kissed him, she'd wanted to lie down with him right there on the grass and make love. Dan had stiffened and pulled away, and though he hadn't said it in so many words, she had sensed his embarrassment. He had never been openly affectionate, and it hadn't occurred to her that he was too inhibited to enjoy their outdoor lovemaking. But he was, and she'd felt an acute humiliation as he'd pulled away.

"What will it take?" Mike asked softly. "Is there anything that will make you trust me?"

"Maybe if you come back," she said, her voice trembling as she tried unsuccessfully to smile. "I've never known anyone like you, Mike. But the only other drillers I knew left a bad taste in my mouth."

He shook his head slowly. "Do you really mistrust me that much, to think I'm like they were? Do you really believe I'm here to take what I can get before I leave for good?"

The indictment in his voice rang through her like a clap of thunder. "I don't know what to think," she said slowly. "All I know is that I hurt inside. And I'm afraid I'm going to hurt a lot more if you turn out to be some kind of mirage." There. She'd laid her vulnerability before him like a freshly cut flower.

"Cally." His finger stroked down her cheek. "Is it commitment you want? Do you want me to tell you I love you?"

"Don't," she pleaded, tears springing to her eyes. She would accept anything to assuage her hurt, even a lie, and she couldn't take the chance he might tell her one.

A long silence stretched between them, and she held her breath, waiting for him to speak.

"Let's go back to the house," he said at last, and she heard the finality in his voice. "It wasn't a good day for a picnic after all."

She scraped her legs out to stand up, feeling a strange void when she saw that her shoe had dug across the clump of violets, breaking one of the stems. By morning the flower would be wilted and dead.

It was still dark the next morning, and Cally was shivering in her jeans and sweater in the kitchen as Mike gave her a quick kiss on the cheek. Happy was waiting outside in the red pickup truck that had driven over her wheat field that first day. Mike had insisted on leaving Bunky for her, though Cally had protested.

"Come with me," Mike said suddenly, his hands on her shoulders.

"I can't," she whispered.

"You need to get away from here," he coaxed her. "This rift between us isn't going to go away here on the farm, Cally, and you know it."

"I can't," she repeated, a catch in her voice. "Don't ask me right now. Please."

"All right." A swift smile touched his face. "Not now. But I will ask again, Cally. Not too many times though." The last was a soft warning, and she understood.

"Take care, Mike."

She bit her lip as he walked out the door, wondering if she was seeing him for the last time.

Chapter Seven

THE BUCYRUS ERIE conspired against Cally all week. In Cally's mind it was acting like a spoiled child, pouting because Mike had left. Cally was three hundred feet down when the shale collapsed again on the bit, and she lost three days and most of her patience fishing it out again. Cally chalked that up to bad luck, but when the drill was finally operational and the bail bucket jammed, she was sure it was all a conspiracy.

She drove into town to pick up a new piece for the dart valve, stoically refusing to take Bunky. The way she saw it, it was a matter of principle. But principle didn't get her back home after Daffy took ill halfway there and dumped the contents of its radiator all over the road. At that point she was feeling a bit queasy herself. It had to be purely coincidental that everything was going wrong now that Mike had left, she told herself halfheartedly as she rode back home with Alma Thornton. Alma was seventy-five years old and barely cleared the steering wheel, even if you counted the two inches of her neatly coiled white bun. "You shouldn't be hitchhiking, Cally," Alma lectured her. "It isn't safe."

"Thank you, Miss Thornton," Cally said automatically, glancing surreptitiously at the speedometer. Thirty miles an hour. At this rate she wouldn't get home until next week.

No wonder Alma's trips to town were so infrequent. They practically qualified as vacations.

"I just got my hair done," Alma said, shooting an admiring look into the rearview mirror. "Clovis Darnell was there." She lowered her birdlike voice to a confidential tone. "She bleaches her hair, you know. Everyone talks behind her back about how blue it is. But the poor thing must not realize that. By the way, I heard you were keeping company with a young man who's drilling for John."

"We're just friends," Cally said quickly. Word sure traveled fast. Mr. René ought to start issuing press releases in between dying strands of Clovis Darnell's hair blue.

Alma turned the car up Cally's drive. "Now I'll wait here until you get in safely, dear."

"Thank you, Miss Thornton. But really I'll be all right. It's four in the afternoon. The only living creatures around here who might attack me are the pigs."

"You can't be too careful, dear."

Cally gratefully escaped the car after another five-minute lecture on the inadvisability of a woman running a farm alone. She all but collapsed on a kitchen chair, staring balefully at the mail. Nothing but bills, magazine renewal notices, and a supposedly irresistible offer for a free pair of panty hose if she bought one with the enclosed coupon. Nothing from Mike. It was useless to hope anyway. He was busy. He didn't have time to write a letter. Well, he could at least call, she thought peevishly. That is, if he was still thinking about her.

Giving up on that train of thought, she stood up resolutely and went to the phone to call Harley's brother Joe, who ran a gas station. Maybe he could find time to tow Daffy home before dark.

She came down with a spring cold the next morning. She figured her week was just about complete as she sneezed violently and didn't grab the tissue in time. "Lousy code," she muttered in a voice two octaves lower than usual. "All out of asbirin, too."

The phone rang jarringly close to her ear, and for a moment she wondered if word of her cold had already spread to the pharmacy and Mr. Bartlett.

"Hello?"

A split second of silence, then, "Cally, is that you?"

Mike! He'd finally called. "Ob course it's me. Who else would answer the phone at this hour?"

"You sound awful, honey. Have you got a cold?"

"No, I like to sleep with a clothespin on my nose."

"I'll have to file that away for future reference," he said softly, and she felt warm blood suffusing her face. If she didn't have a fever when she answered the phone, she had one now. "Who's taking care of you?" Mike asked.

"Who's taking care of *me?*" she repeated in annoyance. "I'm worried about who's going to take care of the hogs. I've got to get to the store for feed this morning."

"No, you don't. You stay right there in bed."

"Are you going to feed my hogs long distance, Donovan?"

"It's so sexy the way you say my name," he retorted. "Now forget about the hogs. I'll arrange everything."

"How the heck are you going to—?"

"Don't bother your stuffed-up head with details," he interrupted. "Just get some rest, and then come see me."

That caught her off guard, and it was a moment before what he'd said penetrated her befuddled brain. "Come see you?"

"Yes. That's what's known in polite circles as a blatant invitation. Come to St. Louis." His tone became low and coaxing on the last, and she sniffled.

"I can barely get out of bed, much less go to St. Louis." But there was regret in her voice.

"When you feel better," he whispered. "I have the perfect cold cure. It involves the use of a bed and warm massage by a member of the opposite sex."

"Good old Doc Donovan," she murmured, mopping her suddenly hot brow.

His low chuckle brought a new wave of feverish heat to her blood. "Come down for the cure, honey."

"Not now, Mike," she managed to get out between two sneezes.

"Of course, love. Come down whenever you're back to normal." There was a slight pause. "I'll complete your cure myself."

"Donovan!" she protested as she blew her nose. "You're driving me crazy."

"Good. Then we're even. Now get some sleep. Bye, Cally."

Smothering a yawn, Cally dropped the receiver in the general direction of the phone cradle and lay back. Fumbling for a handful of tissues, she stuck them against her nose just as the next two sneezes exploded. The hogs could wait for another hour, she decided. They weren't going to starve while she tried to get just a little more sleep.

She didn't know how long she dozed, but when she opened her eyes the sun had topped the edge of the wheat field and was spilling into the bedroom. The clanging of the hog feeders brought her wide awake. She heard a truck and went to the window to check the feedlot. There was John, standing in the back of his pickup, emptying feed sacks into the conical metal hog feeder. No doubt this was Mike's handiwork, and for once she didn't resent his interference.

Half an hour later Cally heard a car in the drive, and when she saw Donna's Trans Am she figured she was having a relapse. "Hello," Donna called cheerily as she mounted the stairs. "I bring greetings and tiny time pills."

Donna popped her head in the door and held up a paper bag. "This has to be an apparition," Cally mumbled, shaking her head slowly. "Obviously I'm running a high fever and hallucinating. Donna cannot be here in the flesh before nine in the morning."

"Ungrateful wretch," Donna chided her. "But I'll chalk it up to your illness. Besides, I talked to your Mike Donovan, and I think he's divine."

"He engineered all this, didn't he?" Cally said.

"If you mean the man with the sexy voice, yes, he certainly did." Donna smiled brightly. "Do you know he called John Masters to take over your menu planning or whatever it is you do for those pigs and cows, and he got my number from him. He was calling from a pay phone, and the operator kept interrupting for more money. He must have fed a fortune into that phone. It was so romantic!"

"He's taking over my life again," Cally groaned, sniffling, "and he's over a hundred miles away."

"You're just feeling sorry for yourself," Donna said. "Here, take a cold capsule and I'll fix you something to eat."

"Don't want to eat," Cally muttered.

"You sound just like Timmy did when he was two," Donna said with a shake of her head. "I used to bribe him with ice cream. Well, I can always give it a shot."

Cally groaned and burrowed under the covers.

Donna insisted on making Cally some kind of French pancakes that she learned to prepare in one of her gourmet cooking classes. She told Cally she couldn't find any curaçao for the orange sauce, so she'd substituted some of the brandy she found in the cupboard. Cally stopped Donna just as she was about to hold a match to the sauce.

"But it looks so pretty flaming," Donna protested.

"I really don't think I could swallow anything that's been on fire at the moment," Cally explained diplomatically. After tasting the crepes, she wondered if maybe they might have been more palatable after a fire. Apologizing that her appetite wasn't itself, she turned instead to the bowl of chocolate ice cream Donna had brought.

"By the way," Donna said, flipping a piece of paper onto the bed. "This is from Mike."

Cally picked up the paper, frowning. "What's this?"

"Directions to his house. He told me to write them down for you. He said he's going to have a week's break or so from his current job in a few days."

"I'm not going to St. Louis," Cally said emphatically, taking another spoonful of ice cream.

"That's just the cold medicine talking," Donna said smugly.

Four days later Cally was feeling much better; so much better, in fact, that she decided she was up to doing her own chores. She opened her closet door to find a clean blouse and stared at Dan's shirts and pants hanging there. Mike's angry words rang out as clearly as the day he spoke them, and Cally blanched. She started to pull out her blouse, then stopped. Resolutely she took Dan's clothes from their hangers and began stacking them on the floor. It was time she made a trip to the Salvation Army.

The next afternoon, Cally asked John to do the feeding and watering a few more days. She pocketed the directions to Mike's house, threw her suitcase in the new truck, and took off as the sun was setting.

A few hours later she was entering the St. Louis city limits on I-70. She took the exit Donna had written down and frowned. This was taking her into the city. Surely Donna had made some mistake.

She reread the directions again as she pulled to a stop in front of the address Donna had written on the paper and shook her head. She was parked a stone's throw from the Gateway Arch and the stadium, in the shadow of a twenty-story apartment building. There had to be some mistake.

Maybe Mike had an office here. She pulled the truck into a parking garage on the same block and smoothed her skirt as she got out of the truck. She was wearing a lavender skirt with a front kick-pleat, a matching jacket in a short box style and a dark plum blouse. She'd made the suit herself three years ago. Her hair was down, but pulled back with a lavender ribbon, and she wore light makeup, just blusher and mascara.

Hesitantly she went through the large glass doors of the apartment building. "May I help you, ma'am?" a uniformed doorman asked deferentially.

"I'm looking for Mike Donovan," she said.

"Fifteen twelve," he said, tipping his hat. "If you'll leave your name I'll buzz him and let him know you're on your way."

"Cally Taylor," she said after a slight pause. She was tempted to turn around and head back to Prairie Junction. This whole thing was beginning to make her nervous. She thought Mike would have a small house somewhere in the country, his drill rigs lined up in back. This glass-and-concrete monster wasn't a home. It had to be Mike's office.

The elevator buzzed her to the fifteenth floor in a matter of seconds. Soundlessly the door opened, and Cally stepped cautiously into a hall dimly lit with recessed lights. One wall was lined with glass, reflecting the thick blue carpeting. She took a deep breath, more and more unsure of herself.

"Cally!" Mike emerged from a large door at the end of the hall and bounded toward her. For a moment she couldn't think of anything but how good it was to see him again, and she hurried toward him. He caught her to him and lifted her up, spinning her in a circle. "I can't tell you how I've missed you," he murmured against her hair. "The nights have been pretty lonely, honey."

She offered him a dazed smile as he set her down, then frowned as she took in what he was wearing—a tuxedo with a stark white shirt that had a front ruffle and pearl studs. Shyly she backed up a step. "I should have called," she said apologetically. "I came at a bad time."

He laughed deep in his throat, his eyes moving over her hungrily. "Your timing's perfect. I was slowly going crazy not seeing you."

She eyed his tux. "You're entertaining tonight?"

"Just a little business get-together. Come on in, and I'll introduce you."

Cally hung back, but Mike put his arm around her waist and drew her toward the apartment. When he opened the door she heard low music and subdued voices. She felt out of place as soon as she stepped inside. She was nearly knee-deep in white carpeting, facing an open kitchen with white-tiled counters and starkly dramatic black-tiled walls. Copper-bottomed pots hung from a beam over a butcher-block worktable. A serving counter faced the living room, and a glass rack filled with sparkling wineglasses was suspended over the counter. She assumed the hall to the left led to the bedrooms. Mike was guiding her to the right, toward the voices. Cally moved stiffly, taking in the large room with its air of spaciousness. Glass windows dominated two walls, and Cally sucked in her breath as a panoramic view of city lights and the gleaming Gateway Arch unfolded before her. A white modular sofa made a half-circle around a glass coffee table on which a delicate ceramic bowl filled with white rosebuds and baby's breath was displayed. And five people in evening clothes stood or sat around the table, holding drinks. Low conversational murmurings were interspersed with the clink of ice against glass.

Three men and two women turned as Mike propelled Cally forward. She acknowledged the introductions and polite smiles and took a seat near the end of the couch. Mike stood beside her, his hand on her shoulder as he discussed a new oil field in southern Illinois with one of the men. Everyone there was connected with an oil company in one way or another. The tall, portly man with wings of gray in his hair was the regional director of a major company. One of the women was his wife. The others were single: the two men worked as geologists for another company, and the woman was a petroleum engineer.

Mike brought Cally a glass of white wine on the rocks, and she sat perched on the edge of the couch, smiling woodenly as the petroleum engineer talked about her last trip to South America to oversee a drilling project. "Are you in the oil business?" she asked Cally, and Cally coughed on an ice cube.

"In a way," she hedged.

"Do you work for Mike?"

"No, I'm self-employed."

There was a moment of silence, and the woman asked incredulously, "You own your own company?"

Cally gave her a wry smile. "Not really. I do some drilling with a Bucyrus Erie."

"Isn't that a churn drill?" the woman asked, and Cally could see her recoiling slightly.

Cally nodded. "It was my grandfather's."

"Well, aren't you the little trouper," the woman said, giving Cally a fixed smile. "I guess you don't have to worry about the hard work with Mike around to help you."

"No," Cally said shortly. "Not a worry."

It was after midnight when Mike's guests began to leave, and Cally remained fixed to the sofa even after the last person, the petroleum engineer, exited, her lace stole capping a black silk cocktail dress.

When Cally looked up from her glass, Mike was standing before her, his arms extended. "Come here," he whispered, his lips twisting in a taut smile. "It's been too long."

She let him draw her to her feet and enfold her in a tender embrace, but she shifted her weight uneasily, pliant but reserved.

She saw the puzzlement in his eyes when he held her away. "What's wrong?" he asked.

Cally swung her eyes away from him and fixed her gaze on the vase of roses. She crossed her arms, massaging her upper arms with her fingertips. Slowly Mike withdrew his hands from her shoulders, and from the corner of her eye she saw him unbutton his jacket and loosen his tie.

She touched one of the roses delicately. "These are beautiful. Did you arrange them yourself?"

"No. There's a little flower shop around the corner, and the clerk fixed these for the get-together."

"A get-together is a barbecue with everyone wearing cutoffs, or a bunch of people plunking down on the floor to eat pizza, drink beer, and watch a football game. This"— she swept her hand quickly around the room—"this was a gala event."

"It wasn't gala until you got here," he said softly.

"Does my visit really rate roses?"

"Cally, if I'd known you were coming tonight I'd have covered the bed with flowers. Now what's wrong?" His voice was still gentle, but she caught the thread of impatience.

"I wasn't prepared for this."

"For what?"

She swung back to him and reached her hand out to touch one of the pearl studs on his shirt. "If you recall, the only times I've seen you, you've been wearing flannel shirts and jeans. You drive a pickup. You eat hamburgers."

Mike sighed and caught her hand in his, pressing it to his chest. "And you arrive here and find me looking like Mr. Peanut." His eyes narrowed as he scrutinized her. "I can't see a minor detail like that throwing you for a loop, Cally. You're too sure of yourself for that. What gives? Was it the party?"

Slowly she withdrew her hand from his and jammed it into her jacket pocket. She couldn't form coherent thoughts when she could feel his heart beating in a rhythm that beckoned her closer. "I love parties," she said with false brightness. "All the chit-chat, the hors d'oeuvres. The elegant clothes. Why, I wish I'd known; I have this super polyester pantsuit I wore to the Prairie Junction Groundhog Day dance..."

"Stop it, Cally." His voice was sharp and commanding. "I don't buy this poor country girl act. It's not you."

"Well, I'm sorry," she said, her voice rising, "but I

happen to feel like the country mouse here. And you live in the city."

"I'm the same person whether I'm dressed in jeans or a tux," he said in a calm, controlled voice that turned her cold. She sensed that he could be deadly when he was angry. "I gave you credit for realizing that, and for that reason I didn't forewarn you about the apartment or what I might happen to be wearing or about what type of people might or might not be visiting."

"*Forewarn* is a good choice of words," she retorted. "When you opened the door I felt like I'd stepped onto another planet. You blithely waltzed me in here and— boom—I was in the middle of a fancy cocktail party with people in theater clothes who control most of the oil in this country."

He jerked off his tie and tossed it on the couch. "What's the issue here?" he demanded. "Those people were here because I've invested quite a bit of money with them. I think the problem is that I have that kind of money to invest. That apparently threatens you."

"All right," she rejoined angrily, taking a step back to glare at him. "It does bother me that you have money, as you put it. You lied to me by not telling me." She ignored his derisive snort and took a deep breath. "You showed up at my house looking like everyone else in Prairie Junction, a hard-working man, and I took that at face value. This"— she gestured around the room, her last movement including him—"wasn't part of the bargain."

"*This* is part of me, Cally." His voice was low, and he appeared more regretful than angry now. "I'm the same man I was in Prairie Junction, just as you're the same woman you were there. I won't apologize for what I am, Cally. I never have. And I do work hard for my money." He went to the small bar built into the end of the counter and poured himself another drink. "Actually I've been thinking about selling this place." Slowly he faced her and took a sip of his drink. "Marcia picked it out."

She fumbled on the coffee table for her own wineglass and took a hasty swallow. When she didn't speak, he said, "Do you want to hear it all, Cally?"

It wasn't a question of wanting now. She had to hear it.

She had to find a way to come to terms with the man Mike was, past and present. Otherwise, they would never breach this impasse.

"Yes," she said softly, cradling the wineglass.

He paced the room for a moment and stopped in front of her. "When Marcia and I married, she had just broken up with another man. But apparently she hadn't forgotten him. I was working hard to get the drilling business going, and in four years I had it to a point where I was doing well. Marcia wanted to move to the city, to this apartment. Since I was gone a lot, I thought, well, why not? She wouldn't be so alone." He stopped and stared down into his glass, gently shaking the ice cubes together. "I found out a year later that she wasn't exactly alone. She entertained her old boyfriend when I was gone."

"I'm sorry," Cally whispered.

"It seems she wanted the best of both worlds," Mike said, his eyes rising to hers and impaling them with startling clarity. "She wanted this world of money, and she wanted the one with her boyfriend. She finally made her choice two months later when her boyfriend got an executive position with a large company. She divorced me."

"Mike," she began in a quiet voice, but he held up his hand to silence her.

"Since that time," he said dryly, "I've had little tolerance for anyone who is incapable of making a choice." He raised his glass to his lips, and Cally's hand tightened. She knew what he was telling her. Her choice was between him and Dan's memory. Mike couldn't make a commitment to her as long as she remained tied to the farm.

"It's ironic, isn't it," she said with a humorless twist of her lips. "One woman needed the security of your money, and another feels threatened by it."

"Very ironic," he agreed softly.

After a long silence during which he watched her over the rim of his glass, she said, "Well, what do you propose we do about this? Should I do the tactful thing and get myself back to Prairie Junction with utmost speed?"

She saw the first slight smile he'd shown since the argument had begun. "No," he said softly. "I think you ought to get some sleep. We'll work this out in the morning. Come on. Give me your keys, and I'll bring up your things."

When he returned he showed her to a cozy bedroom off the hall and put her suitcase on the chair. "I won't ask you if Marcia decorated this room," Cally said wryly. She liked the room with its warm paneling, earth-tone rug, and the daybed with cheerful yellow upholstery.

"No." He smiled at her. "I fixed this up as my den. I thought you'd be more comfortable here than . . . with me, much as . . . well—"

She nodded primly. "Thank you," she said, though her heart sang with regret.

"The bathroom is just across the hall. I have to run some errands in the morning, so if I'm not here when you get up I'll be right back."

She glanced back into the living room after she'd showered and put on her nightgown. There was a single light burning, and Mike sat on the couch, his back to her. His jacket was flung over the back of the couch, and his cuffs were undone. He was still holding the drink in his hand, but he seemed to be studying it, and Cally silently withdrew.

Chapter Eight

SHE SLEPT UNEASILY that night, partly from the muffled noise of traffic below and partly from the knowledge that she was fifteen stories up in the air. Or was it fourteen? She'd read somewhere that skyscrapers didn't have thirteenth floors. At any rate, she was a lot higher than the second-floor bedroom of the farmhouse. She berated herself for being an incurable hick. But it was impossible to sleep without the lullaby of the pigs banging the feeders and the wind rustling through the fields.

She woke up in the morning at sunup and resolutely pulled the sheet back over her head. She might be a hick, but she wasn't stupid enough to get up at the crack of dawn if she didn't have to. Maybe Donna had the right idea after all.

When she awoke again it was late, almost noon, and she slid out of bed guiltily. She looked out the window at the traffic below and took a deep breath.

She would need all of her inner resources to deal with this remaining wall between her and Mike, this barrier of mistrust on her part and impatience on his. She had gleaned from his face last night that she would have to make a decision.

She was just brushing her hair when she heard the door

open as he came into the apartment. Just the sound of his light tread on the carpeting made her mouth go dry, and she gave herself one last check in the mirror. She was wearing a soft brown skirt and a bright red polo shirt and espadrilles. Expecting that they'd be walking in the city today, she quickly tied her hair at the nape of her neck and anchored it with a red comb.

When she saw him in the kitchen she stopped short and stared. He was dressed the way he always did when he was drilling, jeans and a flannel shirt, this one a blue-and-green plaid that set off his dark blue eyes.

"Good afternoon," he said cheerfully, giving her a warm smile. "Want some coffee?"

She nodded, still taken aback. She took the cup from him and watched as he opened a bread box and took out a bakery bag. "I got some Danish, if you're hungry."

They both reached for the napkins at the same time, and she froze when his hand touched hers. Neither of them moved as Mike's hand closed over her smaller one. His thumb stroked her palm as he brought her hand to his lips and kissed her fingers. "I don't think Danish is going to do much toward satisfying my appetite," he said with a husky laugh, and Cally felt her pulse leap to life. Danish wasn't going to help her much either. The tension had mounted in her since she first woke up. She was finally learning it was all right to feel this singing desire for his touch, to want him after only a glance. She closed her eyes heavily as he opened her hand and kissed the palm. Her body strained toward him of its own accord. He clasped her hand against his chest as he pulled her against him. His mouth possessed hers with a need that fueled her own heated response. She was rapidly turning into soft butter beneath his touch, and if he continued kissing her like this she was going to dissolve to the floor. The kiss ended so gently and sweetly that her eyes were moist with the ache of wanting him.

He kissed her hand again, and his breath was uneven on her fingers. "If I don't stop now," he murmured with a soft smile, "you're going to be the first course this morning."

She returned his smile shakily. "Maybe I'd better eat that Danish. For some reason my appetite is raging."

She moved to the other side of the counter with her coffee

and roll and sat down, watching him. Tall and lean, he moved with catlike ease even in the small confines of the kitchen. He must have felt her eyes on him, because he looked up suddenly, and the expression on his face as he stared back made breathing difficult.

She could see his fingers moving restlessly on the counter before he turned back to the large paper bag he was packing with food. She could still feel the imprint of his body against hers, and it was as though they were touching, hip to hip, hand to hand. Each time he moved she felt a tug, as though an invisible web of steel threads ran between them. Cally toyed with her roll, her appetite focused only on Mike.

Every few minutes his movements stilled, and he stopped to look at her. It gave her a strange sense of power over him. There was an exhilaration in this, and for the first time in her life she was acutely aware of herself as a woman— a woman with needs and desires.

He stopped working again and sighed. Moving to stand opposite her at the counter, he leaned his forearms on either side of his coffee cup and growled deep in his throat. "What I'm seeing in your face is driving me crazy, lady," he muttered with frustration.

"What are you going to do about it?" she teased him, knowing her hunger for him was written in her smile.

He drummed his fingers on the counter as her smile broadened. "Oh, Cally," he groaned. Snapping his fingers, he snatched up an empty grocery bag from the counter and in one swift movement plopped it over her head. "There," he said triumphantly. "Temptation is out of sight."

Cally giggled from inside the bag. "Now I know how a head of lettuce feels."

"This will never work," Mike said severely as he plucked the bag from her head. "Now I can't take my eyes off the rest of you."

"You're turning into an incorrigible lecher," she said with a shake of her head.

"There's a cure, you know."

"Surgery?"

"You have a sadistic streak, you know that? Be quiet, or I'll put the bag back on your head."

"There is one other cure that I can think of," she said

softly. "Let's see now. As the doctor told me on the phone . . ."

He touched her hair, his fingertips sliding down to stroke her neck. "I had that in mind," he whispered. "But not here."

"Not here?" she repeated in confusion. "I don't understand."

"Not for our first time," he said gently. "I have a better place in mind. In fact, if you're ready we can leave."

"Leave? Whatever are you talking about?"

"Trust me." His bantering tone gave way to a quiet seriousness as he repeated, "Trust me."

And trust him she did. She refrained from asking any more questions during the hour-long drive south on I-55. "This feels positively decadent," she commented when they had long since left the city limits and were passing fewer houses and more rolling hills on the Interstate. "I'm being taken out of the city for illicit purposes. I bet we're going to some lovely rustic chalet with a roaring fireplace and satin sheets."

His sideways glance was amused. "Well, you got the rustic part right. I hope they taught you basic survival in 4-H."

Now *that* worried her, and she ruminated on his comment the rest of the trip. Her only basic survival skill was the ability to identify poison ivy. Her thoughts began turning to more primitive abodes than chalets. A cabin maybe?

Reality, once again, was not what she expected. Mike turned the truck off the Interstate and onto a county road identified only by two letters, MM. "Was this road named for the candy or did whoever's in charge of naming roads run out of names when he got to this one?"

He just smiled and kept his eyes on the road, which wound past a stream. He turned off at a narrow gravel road that said PRIVATE DRIVE, and Cally looked around at the stands of cedars on either side of the road. "Rustic, you said," she murmured in an undertone. It seemed they had gone at least two miles on the bumpy gravel road when Mike stopped the truck. Cally looked around. They were in a small valley, totally surrounded by trees. She could hear running water nearby. She turned to him with a straight face and asked, "Is this where you bring your lady friends to park?"

"Only the ones who accuse me of lechery." He looked at her with an exaggerated lift of his eyebrows and an evil grin. "I have you now, my lovely."

"You've been watching too many bad movies," she said, shaking her head. His eyes were glowing, and Cally felt a shiver of anticipation as she lost herself in his gaze.

"Come on," he said, taking her hand. "I want you to see the place." He helped her out on his side and stopped to look around. It was a beautiful day, and the afternoon sun was casting lazy warmth everywhere. A single yellow butterfly danced in a shaft of sunlight before flitting off to the wild flowers in the shade of the trees. Beyond a small hill she could hear young frogs peeping energetically. The hills were a subtle purple-green hue peculiar to stands of cedars, and where the sun touched a distant pond the light reflected with the radiance of a fine diamond.

"It's lovely," Cally said softly.

"I bought fifty acres here several years ago, mainly as an investment, but the place grew on me. I'm hoping to build in the future. See that pond? I've stocked it with catfish. Eventually I'd like to raise some trout here, too. There's a good-size stream in that direction." He jammed his hands into his pockets and exhaled slowly. "I hope you like camping out."

"You know," she said, glancing around, "I used to dream about a place like this when I was little. I'd lie in bed at night in the summer. I slept in the second-story bedroom, and we didn't have air conditioning. There was a window fan, but it was pretty noisy. Anyway, I'd lie there awake and wish I had a place to go that only I knew about. There would be lots of trees and a cool stream, and I'd lie down there." Her voice trailed off, and she turned to look at him. Mike took her hand and squeezed it.

"Do you mind that you're not the only one who knows about this place?" he asked softly.

She shook her head decisively. "In my dream it was a lonely place. The reality is much better."

"Tell you what," Mike said. "Why don't you go exploring while I get things set up here?"

"Can I help?"

"No, lovely lady. I want you to go look for all the good places to plant flowers. I'm appointing you head gardener."

"Ah, a challenge," she said. "All right. I'll go plan the landscaping. See you later."

She began walking through the trees to the stream he'd indicated. The water was rolling lazily over stones and gravel, and she estimated the depth to be about two feet. It looked so inviting that she sat down on the bank and took off her shoes, dangling her feet over the water. She tested the water with one toe and immediately withdrew her foot. Icy cold. Just the way she'd imagined it in her dream.

She let her gaze wander lazily downstream, where there was a bend, and then she saw the perfect spot for a house. Right where the stream made a gentle turn there was a large, old willow tree leaning over the water, one root protruding from the bank like a crooked finger. A few yards behind the willow was where the house should go. The ground swelled up a grassy slope, but then it leveled off to a perfect location. The house would overlook the stream with the hills rising gently behind it. She could see beds of red tulips and white hyacinths in the front, with phlox leading down the slope to the stream. In the front there would be a large picture window with boxes of bright red geraniums. And in the back a rose garden. With a start it dawned on her that she was planning the house and flowers as though she were going to be living there. She sat very still, afraid to move, because she didn't want to face this new revelation. For once that nagging voice inside her head was silent—no doubt at a complete loss for words.

She lay back on the bank and studied the patches of blue sky visible through the latticework of tree branches overhead. If she was waiting for some earthshaking discovery, it didn't come. She closed her eyes and imagined the farm in Prairie Junction, and she felt a pang. Right now it seemed less like home than this piece of bank where she was lying. Even Dan's memory seemed alien here. It was still a part of her, but not an all-consuming part, eating away at her heart. Perhaps she'd finally put her marriage into perspective.

She must have fallen asleep as her thoughts drifted, because she woke slowly to find a butterfly perched on her hand. Her sudden movement sent the butterfly flitting away, and Cally glanced overhead. The sun was beginning its descent in the west. Gradually she rolled over and stretched and stood up, brushing off her skirt.

She walked back to the clearing and stopped in surprise when she saw that Mike had pitched a small tent and had a fire going in front of it.

"Quite the busy homemaker you are," she said, walking toward him.

"I thought we ought to have a roof over our heads, so to speak. Did you enjoy your walk?"

She nodded. "I fell asleep by the stream. There's a beautiful spot there at the stream's bend—" Her enthusiasm died out as she stopped in mid-sentence. She looked at the ground guiltily.

He waited a moment, then said, "It is beautiful there. I think I'd like my bedroom overlooking the stream."

She nodded, trying not to think of the house and the flower beds and his bedroom.

He took her for a short walk to the pond and back, and then they started dinner. Cally rubbed the steaks with garlic before Mike laid them in the skillet. He had brought salads and beer in a cooler, and garlic bread that they wrapped in foil and rewarmed over the coals.

She sat down on the blanket opposite him, curling her legs under her. They set their plates on a small wooden table he'd produced from the back of the truck, and Mike sat crosslegged, his eyes lingering on her. She ran her hand over the nappy surface of the soft brown blanket, her mind drifting back to the bank where she'd fallen asleep and the house she'd imagined there.

"Aren't you hungry?" he asked.

"Yes, very," she said quickly, swinging her attention back to him, coloring as she met his steady gaze. Hurriedly she lowered her eyes and began eating. They made small talk, but Cally could think of little other than the man across from her.

When they finished, it was getting late, and dusk was falling like a misty veil over the valley. Crickets chirped in answer to the chorus of frogs in the pond, and a light breeze sprang up as the moon rode high in the trees.

"Time for dessert," Mike announced, standing up to set their dishes aside. From the cooler he produced two plastic containers. "Fresh strawberries and a choice sponge cake. Put them together with a little whipped cream, and instant heaven."

"Want another beer?" Cally asked, holding one up.

"Sounds good. Be sure you don't open the one that—"

She snapped open the tab before he finished, and there was an explosion of foam. In the moment she stood there in surprise, the beer sprayed her hair, her face, and her polo shirt. By the time she reacted, it had already stopped spewing foam.

"—rolled around the back of the truck," Mike finished, eyeing her apologetically. "Sorry."

"I was wondering what you did when you wanted to shower out here," Cally said gamely. "Now I know." Beer was dripping off her forehead, down her nose and off her chin. Visions of Mike tenderly taking her in his arms in the moonlight dissolved with the bubbles on her shirt. When she came to St. Louis, she knew she was in essence saying, *It's okay. I'm ready now.* She'd even packed her sheer nightie and her lavender teddy, both birthday gifts from Donna. And here she stood smelling like a brewery, beer dripping from her ears and hair and chin. It was not exactly what she'd had in mind.

"Come on," he said, taking her hand. "I've got some water heated up for the dishes. We'll use it on you instead."

The air was nippy, and she shivered as she pulled off her shoes. Mike was dipping a washcloth in the water kettle over the fire, apparently oblivious of the fact that she was hesitant about taking off any more garments right there.

He began to sponge her face and hair, and as she stared back at him, his movements became slower and softer. "You'll have to take everything off," he whispered. His dark, heated gaze remained fixed on her face as he carefully undid her skirt and slipped it over her hips. She stepped out of it, now wearing a very wet shirt and red panties with lace around the legs. He worked up the polo shirt next, his hands brushing her breasts, which stood taut against a red camisole.

She was feeling shivers that had nothing to do with the night air. He closed his eyes tightly, then opened them again, giving her a long, hungry appraisal before his hands lightly stroked her hardening nipples through the silky fabric. With a sense of wonder she realized his hands were trembling as he pulled the red top the rest of the way over her head. It joined her skirt on the ground.

"This is nice," he whispered, running his eyes over the camisole and panties. He reached out and slowly removed the comb at the nape of her neck, fanning her hair out over her shoulders with his hands. One finger hooked a camisole strap and slid it off her shoulder, then the other strap. Languorously, she began unbuttoning his shirt, and he shrugged it off.

She raised her arms as he gently pulled up the camisole. The lacy hem brushed her breasts, further tantalizing her senses. His eyes turned murky as they followed the curves of her body. Swiftly he slid his hand under the waist of the panties and pulled them down. Cally stepped out of them and stood facing him, reveling in the open adoration on his face.

Mike sponged her off with infinite care, his tongue and hands following to dry her moist skin. He kept his eyes fastened on her, as though afraid she'd evaporate into the night air, and Cally had never felt such a sense that she was worshiped.

He kicked off his shoes, then the jeans. "Didn't your mother ever tell you to wear underwear?" she whispered raggedly. "Mine always said, 'What if you were in an accident?'"

He laughed and reached out to pull her against him. "That was one of her standard lectures. She was a first-grade teacher, and all the grade school alumni that passed before her blackboard have that indelibly imprinted on their minds."

"Today's lesson is underwear," Cally continued, burrowing her head against his shoulder, nibbling at his flesh until she heard him groan.

"Today's lesson is outdoor frolicking," he said with

meaning, his hands tightening in her hair. He pulled them both to their knees, his mouth capturing hers on the way down. His coarse chest hair was pressing her breasts, and she leaned against him, twining her arms around his neck. "And what are the requirements of today's lesson?" she said, breathing against his neck, trying to hide her increasing breathlessness.

"Surviving a night in the wild with a man who can't get enough of you." He brought her mouth back to his, his teeth catching and teasing her lower lip until it felt swollen with pleasure. The grass beneath her knees was damp and soft and almost as sweet as the touch of his lips on her face and neck. One hand trailed down her side to her hip and then around to her belly, which quivered under his touch. His hand dipped lower, and she caught her lip in her teeth, her eyes opening and then softly closing on a sigh.

Gently he lay back, drawing her into his arms. He cradled her to him and lowered her onto the blanket where they'd shared dinner. He propped himself up on one elbow, his finger tracing a delicate line over her brow and down her cheek to her lips. She tried to catch his wandering finger in her mouth, but he eluded her, returning to lightly stroke her full lower lip, making her ache for his fuller possession.

"Mike," she whispered, her eyes taking in the uneven cadence of his breathing and the way his flesh silvered in the moonlight.

"Shhh," he whispered back. "I want to remember how you look like this. I've never seen anything so lovely. Besides," he murmured as he bent down to nibble her earlobe, "no talking during class."

In truth, talking was out of the question. She could barely think, and when she did manage to collect her thoughts in between the incredible sensations he was creating in her, she realized she, too, was trying to memorize how he looked and how he moved. She had to remember, because she'd never known anything so exquisite in her life, and she might never know it again.

It was a bittersweet pleasure as he raised her hips to his and she experienced a pressure so intense and sweet that she dug her fingers into his back. He filled her, body and soul, and she accepted him eagerly, giving herself up to him. "Cally," he murmured roughly against her ear. "Don't be a dream. Don't disappear like the moonlight."

The throbbing of his heart melded with her own, and the sigh of the wind in the trees became her breath. She felt her entire body pulsing, as though she and Mike were two rivers crashing together in a crescendo, carrying each other on a current so strong neither could fight it.

He pressed his mouth to her breast, circling it with his tongue, spiraling into the heart of her sensitivity.

Her sinews, nerves, every fiber of her being were stretched taut, singing with electricity. The sparks grew hotter in intensity until they collected to explode in one incredible burst of flame. Each thread of her body burned through and snapped in a shuddering spasm that seemed to send her very soul flying free, upward to the trees and beyond.

She lay in his arms feeling primitive and unfettered. Swimming to the surface of her own lethargy, she dragged her eyes open and studied his face, wanting that for her memories, greedy for every detail she could capture. His arm was cradling her head as he lay beside her, and his shoulder tasted salty against her lips. He opened his eyes and looked at her lovingly, and she read everything she'd ever wanted to see in a lover's gaze. More than merely sated, his blue eyes were hazed with a tender possessiveness. His hand tangled in her hair, and he brought his lips to her forehead, brushing it lightly.

"Did I pass the class?" she whispered, nuzzling his neck.

"Sweetheart," he breathed, "you've passed every class in the school."

She laughed against his throat and turned her face to the sky as Mike pulled the blanket around them. The brilliance of the heavens was matched only by the glow of his eyes. She knew at that moment how a star felt when it was born into the universe, bright and burning.

Chapter Nine

SHE HEARD A noise and woke up in the tent, stretching out her hand to find the other half of the two-person sleeping bag empty. Giggling like a couple of children camping out in the backyard, they'd curled up together in the sleeping bag, after the fire had died down.

She propped herself up on one elbow and looked out the tent flap. He was poking a fire to life in the early morning light. He hadn't bothered to put any clothes on, and she lay back and watched him move easily, like an animal unaware of its natural grace.

He came back into the tent and saw her eyes on him. "Good morning, beautiful," he said, grinning.

"I thought I was dreaming," she murmured, pulling him into her embrace as he crawled back into the sleeping bag. "I thought you might be a marauding wolf out by the fire."

"Ah, but I am, my love," he whispered huskily. "Don't you remember Little Red Riding Hood? The wolf dressed up like her grandmother. Now me, I don't care much for women's clothing—on myself anyway."

"What big eyes you have, Grandmother," she purred seductively.

"All the better to see you with, my dear." He leered.

"What big teeth you have, Grandmother."

"All the better to eat you with, my dear," he growled, nipping her neck.

Giggling, she moved her hand down his chest and over his belly, then lower. "Why, Grandmother," she began, widening her eyes in innocence, "what big ideas you have." She collapsed against him in a gale of laughter as he nuzzled her throat with mock growls.

"You've had it now, Riding Hood," he said with a rise of one dark eyebrow. "And just to be sure no wayward wolves disturb us . . ." He reached into the duffel bag he'd brought and held up a DO NOT DISTURB sign, of the type made to hang on hotel doors. While Cally dissolved in laughter, Mike flipped it over the outside tent flap, then flung himself down beside her, raining kisses all over her face and throat.

They drove back to the city that afternoon, and Cally leaned back against the seat, watching the scenery flash by in dreamy content. She knew why he'd chosen that place—she could only think of it as their place now—for the first time they made love. It was a setting that suited them both, a place where each felt at home. It was wild and beautiful and unrestrained, just like what had happened between them there.

"Ah, inhale that air," Mike said wryly as they pulled into the parking garage by his apartment. "Clean living and lots of chemicals—that's what life's about."

"That and taxes," she added cheerfully.

They carried the camping gear into the elevator with the doorman giving them dignified sideways glances. "What on earth did you tell him when you carried all this stuff to the truck?" she demanded as he unlocked the door.

"I said I was camping out in front of the Cardinals ticket office to get good seats." He gave her a grave look.

Cally dropped her load of gear on the floor just inside the door and impulsively hugged him. "Now I know why they named that road MM," she said softly.

"Oh yeah?"

She nodded solemnly. "It stands for mmmmmm." He

grinned and let his own load of sleeping bags and tent stakes drop to the floor. His arms crushed her against his chest as he returned her kiss.

"You know," he murmured against her hair, "I could order in some food, and we could bar the door and never leave here."

"The doorman might get suspicious." She laughed.

He nodded reluctantly. "I suppose you're right. In that case, how about seeing the sights?"

"As soon as I change," she promised him, glancing ruefully at her beer-stained polo shirt and skirt.

"I thought we'd start with the stadium," he said, taking her arm later as he guided her across the street. They joined a large group there, and Cally held on to Mike's hand as they went through the locker rooms, sportscasters' booths and ended up in the Hall of Fame. "Do you come to the games a lot?" Cally asked, linking her arm in his.

"When I have time." He shrugged. "It was the only thing I really liked about the apartment. It's close to the ball park." He led her along a wall where large black-and-white photos of various Cardinal baseball teams made a montage. He pointed to one young man standing with his arm around another ballplayer in a group picture. "That's my father."

"Your father? Are you kidding?"

"No. He played Triple-A ball for several seasons, and the Cardinals brought him up one year to play second base. He always told me it was the most exciting and the most depressing year of his life."

"What happened?"

"He broke his knee sliding into third base during a regular season game. That ended his playing career."

Cally stared more closely at the man with the same crooked grin as Mike, the same dark hair. "What did he do then?"

"For one thing he lost his sense of humor," Mike said dryly. "I was only a small child when he played ball, but I remember him as a large, laughing man who overnight turned into someone who felt life had passed him by."

"I'm sorry."

"He's a loving father," Mike said, shrugging. "And he

makes a good living with his sporting-goods store. But some of the spark has gone out of him."

They walked outside, and Cally stole sideways glances at Mike. She suspected that whatever piece of humanity had died in Mike's father, it had only strengthened the son.

"What about your mother?" she asked.

"She's a very resilient, resourceful woman," he said, smiling, "and she's provided the humor my father lost. I see them both as often as I can. They live in southern Missouri. And I have a married sister, Lisa, in Minnesota."

"I bet you drove her crazy when you were both little," Cally surmised.

Mike laughed. "Lisa swears I still do. She says her son Jeff is the spit 'n' image of me as a kid."

"They sound nice."

"They are. I think you'll like them." He grabbed her hand and pulled her across the street with him. "Come on. Let's go up in the Arch and look at the waterfront."

Access to the observation windows inside the pinnacle of the Arch turned out to be via minuscule capsules, each with four very crowded seats. Cally climbed in first, squeezing herself against the side, which was windowless. Two older women climbed in next and sat opposite Cally. "What did you think of the brewery tour, Ruth?" one asked the other.

Ruth sniffed. "How you can drink that stuff and at this hour of the day is beyond me."

"Oh, come on," the other said. "When Dad made sour mash, back when we were little, you were the first one out there with a ladle. And you know it, too."

Ruth shook her head primly. "Honestly, Lydia. Living in the city is turning you into a liberal."

Cally suppressed a smile, pressing herself close to the wall as Mike somehow folded his tall frame into the egglike capsule. The door slammed shut, and almost silently the car began its ascent. Cally felt somewhat claustrophobic as the seconds ticked by in silence. "Now I know how a quadruplet feels in the womb," she muttered to no one in particular.

"At least this is a great way to meet women," Mike said, smiling brightly. "It's hard not to be on a first-name basis

when you're practically in each other's arms." He paused
a fraction and added, "Didn't I see you in the stadium?"

Cally nodded. "I'm a sucker for athletes."

"Well, it just so happens that I have a wonderful col-
lection of baseball cards at my apartment. Care to come see
them?" He gave her a lascivious smile.

"I do believe that's a proposition," Cally said demurely.

"Yes, ma'am," he replied solemnly. "It surely is."

The car chose that moment to reach the top of the Arch,
and the door slid open. Cally glanced at the two women.
Ruth was scowling at Mike in obvious disapproval, but
Lydia stared in openmouthed fascination.

The two ladies exited the car with several backward
glances, and Mike and Cally followed, their dignity wrapped
around them like an expensive coat. Cally ran to the windows that lined the opposite wall with an exclamation of
delight. Leaning her hands on the sill, she looked down at
the Mississippi and the boats docked at the foot of the Arch.
Mike came to stand beside her, pointing out various land-
marks. They strolled around the windows, arm in arm, Mike
murmuring things in her ear that were quite inappropriate
for a tour guide.

As they got ready to enter the return capsule, Mike took
Cally's arm and pulled her away from the door. She glanced
at him and saw his devilish grin. When she looked ahead
she saw why. He was leading them to a car occupied by
Ruth and Lydia. Cally slid into the far seat, giving the ladies
a polite smile. Ruth tilted her chin up in censure, and Lydia
swallowed hard.

"I don't believe in long courtships, do you?" Mike asked
conversationally as he uncoiled himself next to her.

Now what was he going to pull on those poor, unsus-
pecting ladies? "I've had little experience with them," Cally
said.

"Take my word for it. They're very frustrating." He
nodded, as if in confirmation, finishing with a self-satisfied
smile.

"That must put quite a strain on your love life," Cally
commented. From the corner of her eye she saw Ruth pull
a handkerchief from her purse. No doubt she was in need
of smelling salts.

"Now, you can help me out in that department," Mike said solemnly.

"Oh?" Cally said.

Mike nodded. "You could marry me." There was a choked gasp from Ruth's direction as the car came to a halt, and Mike's arms encircled Cally, drawing her into a kiss that sent her right back to the top of the Arch. The pressure of his mouth increased, and Cally rocketed through the roof and into the sky over St. Louis.

The sound of several throats clearing brought her back down to ground level. Mike lifted his head, his eyes dancing with laughter, and over his shoulder Cally saw a group of four tourists, cameras dangling from their necks like giant pendants, shifting their feet as they stared into the car. Grinning, Mike took her hand as they exited the car and made their way past four openmouthed stares. "We're doing wonders for the St. Louis tourist business," Mike told her.

They were about to cross the street when Cally spotted Lydia and Ruth getting into an early-model Ford. "Uh-oh," she murmured as Lydia paused and watched them, then moved toward them purposefully. "I feel a scolding heading our way."

"I'll explain everything," Mike said.

"That's all right," Cally said. "I can handle it."

Lydia stopped beside Cally, nervously pushing back her short white hair. "Could I speak to you a moment?" she asked in a frail voice, drawing herself up straight.

Cally nodded, following her a few feet away from Mike.

"Marry him," Lydia said in a low voice.

"What?" Cally said in surprise.

"Marry him," Lydia repeated with a little shake of her head. She patted Cally's arm. "If I were forty years younger I'd marry him myself." Straightening her gloves, Lydia turned and marched back to the car, where Ruth sat primly, apparently checking her makeup in a hand mirror.

"Well, did you get the fifty-cent lecture about propriety?" Mike asked when she joined him.

Cally shook her head. "Quite the opposite. It seems that Lydia likes you."

"See, the woman has taste." He gave her a quick peck

on the cheek. "Come on. Let's go get some dinner before I change my mind and invite Lydia along."

"Men are so fickle." Cally sighed, rolling her eyes at him.

He squeezed her hand and gave her a grin that sent her senses back up the Arch. Calm down, Cally. The proposal wasn't for real. He was only kidding, dummy. Then why was her heart still doing double time?

"Donovan," she groaned when they half-fell into the apartment after dinner. "I could kill you for making me eat that éclair for dessert. I feel like I'm going to burst." She staggered into his arms.

"Go ahead and explode," he teased her in a low voice. "The maid comes on Tuesday."

"Not only are you a lecher," she protested mildly, "but you're a heartless one."

"How do you expect a man to have a heart when you're the one who's stolen it?" He tilted her chin up, and the pulse at the base of Cally's throat beat in wild syncopation as she looked up into his face. How could a face become so intimately etched on her brain in such a short time? She had lived with Dan for four years, and his memory was only a mist now. Don't think about that. She closed her eyes tightly, but Dan's face was gone, now. Instead, her image was of Mike.

Past and present had separated, each taking its rightful place in her mind. For a long time she had lived as though the future were some distant shore she could barely see. Now she had crossed that great swell of water separating her from it, and looking back, she saw that what she left was good, but it was gone. She opened her eyes and looked at the man who'd brought her to this new shore.

His fingers trailed along her cheek and jawbone, tracing the full outline of her lips. "I'm the Tin Man, angel—no heart," he whispered, pressing his chin against the top of her head and enfolding her in his arms.

She let her eyes close heavily and breathed in the musky scent of his skin. Funny, she had wanted him to hold her, but she'd forgotten how to ask. When you were alone, you didn't need anybody, or at least you pretended you didn't. Trouble is, the pretending could erase the reality. . . .

"There's never a wizard around when you need one," she said lightly, slowly disentangling herself from his embrace and looking anywhere but at his face. She jammed her hands into her pockets, a defensive gesture to keep them from straying to his chest, and turned her back to him, taking a deep breath. "There aren't even any yellow-brick roads anymore." She walked toward the living room, focusing on the city lights outside the windows. Turning back from the windows, she inspected the shelves lining the wall opposite the couch.

"Nice stereo," she commented, running her fingers over the oak cabinet. "No TV?"

"Press the button on the wall."

She found the panel of buttons and pressed one at random. A recessed light promptly went off.

"The next one to the right," he said.

She pressed that button, and a panel that appeared to be solid wall slid back, revealing a large-screen television and a shelf with other assorted electronic gadgetry.

"Gosh, I just wondered if you had a TV," Cally said, stepping back to eye the monstrosity. "This is more like a movie screen. Do you sell popcorn in the lobby?" Mike didn't answer, and Cally moved over to inspect the shelf of electronics. "What have we here?" she murmured. "A videotape recorder, complete with camera. Don't tell me. You make movies, too." She snapped her fingers. "I've got it. You're really a big movie producer in disguise researching a film on well drillers." She looked at him tentatively. He'd moved to the couch and loosened his tie. He was watching her without expression, and Cally shrugged. "No, I suppose not," she said. "Let's see now. You don't have kids, so that lets out home movies. Vacation movies?" She shook her head. "I can't see you toting this thing along to Club Med. Maybe you like to film your love conquests. Are there mirrors on the bedroom ceiling?"

Mike tossed his tie on the coffee table and turned those penetrating eyes on her. "It came as a package deal," he said quietly. "I shot a tape of all the apartment furnishings in case of theft. Other than the couple of times my nephew

Jeff has fooled with it, it hasn't been used. Would you like a demonstration?"

When she didn't answer, he gestured toward the couch. "Sit down, and I'll set it up."

She watched as he mounted the camera on a tripod and adjusted it, then inserted a tape cartridge into the machine. He pressed two buttons and walked back to the couch with a microphone. "All set," he said.

"Well, what shall we do?" she asked cheerfully. "Sing or dance? If you have a kazoo I could give my famous rendition of 'Feelings.'"

He eyed her silently a moment, then crossed his legs and turned sideways toward her. "How about a little interview game, since you're in such a whimsical mood? I'll be the interviewer, and you can be the celebrity of your choice."

There was a warning note in his voice that he didn't buy this barbed humor of hers, but Cally's tight smile didn't waver. "In that case," she said, "I want to be someone cool, charming, and utterly above reproach. Betty Crocker." She shook her head. "No. No one ever sees her legs. I know. I'll be Minnie Mouse."

He held up the microphone. "All right, Minnie. Welcome to the show. I understand you're here to promote your new book."

He held the microphone in front of her and off the top of her head she said in a high squeaky voice, "Yes, it's called *My Life with Mickey.*"

"Anything new and revealing in the autobiography?"

Cally gave him a coy look. "Well, he liked to eat cheese in bed. And he never took off his shoes."

"Does the fact that Mickey has become wealthy over the years bother you?"

He had remained solemn throughout the entire "interview," and she warily suspected it was more than a game to him. His expression was making her uncomfortable.

"Of course not." she said, lowering her eyes, her voice only halfheartedly squeaky.

"Then what's troubling you?"

"Look, Mike," she said, glancing at him, "we can stop now. I've seen how the camera works."

He set the microphone down between them and leaned

back against the couch, resting his forearm just inches from her shoulder. "We have to talk. What happened when we came back here tonight?"

"Nothing." The fractional bit of space separating them might as well have been a mile. She couldn't reach across it. *Don't press me,* she wanted to tell him. *I need space, and I need you, and I don't know which I need more. Don't make me choose tonight.*

"As I recall, everything was fine until I started to express how I feel about you. And then suddenly you were gone." His finger grazed her collar before brushing her chin the way someone might touch a sleeping child—delicately, half-afraid of disturbing her. "There was a beautiful, empty shell in the room with me, and the beautiful woman named Cally was so far inside it that I couldn't touch her. What happened, lady?"

Leave it to Mike to cut to the quick without anesthetic. "You don't sugarcoat things, do you?" she said wryly. He didn't apologize, only watched her, waiting for her answer. "I guess I'm not ready to hear what you feel, Mike."

"Because of Dan?" he asked bluntly, an edge to his voice.

She shook her head. "It's too fast, Mike. I think I'm caught in some kind of time warp. A lot has happened in a short period of time. I haven't sorted it out." That was only part of it, but it was the only part she could tell him. He was right that his wealth still made her uneasy. And mixed up in all of this was her fear that things wouldn't work out. She couldn't deal with her own turbulent emotions right now, much less with Mike's feelings.

"All right." He searched her face, and Cally swallowed convulsively. Ironically, she suspected that Mike knew her better than she knew herself, and right now he'd probably guessed that she wasn't telling him everything. When some of the tension left his shoulders she relaxed, secure that he wouldn't press her. "Minnie Mouse," he said lightly, "you're an incredible female. I'm wild about your ears."

"You flatter me, sir," she squeaked. "What do you think of my tail?"

"Ah, my innocent," he said in a low, husky voice, leaning close to nibble on her ear. "If I were to answer that right now, I'd have a blue movie on my hands." He stood up and switched off the recorder. "Now, Minnie, come with me, and I'll tell you just what I think about each and every luscious part of your anatomy." He took her hand and led her down the hall to his bedroom. It was the first time she'd seen it, and she didn't know what to expect when he turned on the light.

What she saw was about the last thing she'd expected. There were flowers everywhere—vases of lilies on the dresser, potted tulips in every corner of the room, hanging baskets of fuchsia at the windows. And then there was the bed. The pillows and spread were entirely covered with roses. "My God," Cally murmured in awe. "It looks like a float in the Rose Bowl parade. Is your florist friend responsible for this?"

"She came in while we were at dinner." Mike's eyes were dancing with brilliant lights as he watched her.

"Donovan, you're absolutely crazy," she said, shaking her head. "You said you'd cover the bed with flowers, and you actually did it." She smiled slowly. "And I love it." She shook her head again. "A bed of roses."

"And since I don't want you getting puncture wounds from the thorns, I'd better get these in some water."

Even using every vase he had in the apartment, there weren't enough, and they ended up floating the roses in a bathtub filled with water. "This is class," Cally said, standing up as they finished the job.

"As I recall, we were about to discuss your anatomy," Mike said, gently pulling her back toward the bedroom.

The perfume of flowers utterly filled the air, and Cally drank it in as she looked around. The room was done in soft earth tones—light brown carpeting, even lighter walls, all accented with touches of muted red and yellow. The bed's headboard was a large bookcase filled with volumes of all variety.

"Come here," Mike whispered, sitting on the bed, his smile warm and inviting. "I've been thinking about you all day. Thinking about how good you taste."

Slowly she walked toward him, her breathing growing shallow as she watched him unbutton his shirt and toss it aside. He stood up and began to undress her, slowly and sensually, his eyes dark and sweet with emotion. Her knees trembled under the force of his gaze, and she rested her hands on his bare shoulders to steady herself. The muscle and sinew moved beneath her palms, making her veins throb in passionate response.

He let her halter dress slide to the floor and leaned back to survey her lavender teddy. "Honey," he whispered, "you look good enough to eat. Like a lace-covered sugarplum."

She was trembling from head to toe, despite a delicious warmth that sparked into flames under his kindling gaze. He slid the straps from her shoulders, his fingers lingering on her arms before they traced a delicate line along the lace edge barely covering the rising swell of her breasts. With one finger he pulled down the teddy, communicating his hunger with his eyes before lowering his mouth to taste her creamy flesh. "Sweet," he whispered hoarsely, "so sweet. Your skin's like honey."

She clasped her hands in his hair, and just before she squeezed her eyes shut she focused on the banks of flowers opposite the bed. Tears pricked her eyes and she gasped to hold them at bay. She'd cried once because she wanted daffodils, and her husband didn't give them to her. Now she cried because this man gave her a whole roomful of flowers without her asking.

He raised his head and immediately frowned. "You're crying," he murmured, troubled. "What's wrong, honey?" Gently he wiped away her tears with his finger, then kissed the moist path they'd made.

"It's so good," she choked out. "It's so . . . right." And it was. He pulled her onto his lap, his fingers sliding up the leg of the teddy to explore the tender flesh of her thighs and beyond, making her gasp and clutch his back in rising desire. Every touch was as sweet and perfect as flowers at the height of bloom. She opened to him like a rose to the sun, petals of soft, silky flesh wanting him. Honeyed nectar pounded through her veins, drawing him into her sweet center.

The teddy was on the floor beside his pants as he drew her down on top of him. The bed still bore the scent of roses, and as her hair fell like a curtain around her face, she dipped her mouth to his and drank from the river of pleasure.

His movements and caresses unleashed her own dormant passion, and when he whispered her name hoarsely against her ear she answered him, murmuring his name with mounting emotion, her voice seeming to come from a long distance. The tension and pleasure built until, like a whirlpool, they imploded, drawing the universe through her like a windstorm.

The tremulousness of lovemaking gave way to a dreamlike state through which she was reborn into the warm cocoon of Mike's arms. Love words sang in her head, a rhapsody that faded to a hum as she fell asleep.

It was another kind of humming that woke her up. Blissfully relaxed after the night before, she became dimly aware of low voices. The next thing she noticed when she opened her eyes was a small boy peering at her from the side of the bed. Her immediate reaction was to clutch the bedspread to her neck. A quick glance down reminded her that she'd slipped back into the teddy during the night. She breathed a sigh of relief and smiled at the boy. His dark hair and blue eyes were familiar, and she broke into a grin.

"I'll bet you're Jeff, aren't you?"

He nodded solemnly. "What are you doing in Uncle Mike's bed?" he demanded.

Cally was saved from an indelicate answer as the humming voices in the other room suddenly ceased, and a worried woman's voice called, "Jeff, where are you?"

"In here," he called back, still staring at Cally.

The woman's plaintive groan was accompanied by Mike's laughter. "Oh, my lord," the woman muttered, and Cally heard her footsteps on the carpeting.

A moment later a perky face topped with curly blond hair peered cautiously into the bedroom, and the woman smiled in chagrin. "I'm sorry," she said to Cally. "I'm Jeff's mother, Lisa." She gave the boy a grim frown. "Jeff, you were told to stay out of the bedroom."

"How come Uncle Mike's bathtub is filled with flowers?" Jeff asked.

"Just like his uncle," Lisa said. "If he doesn't have a ready excuse, he changes the subject."

"Unfair," Mike protested, coming to stand beside his

sister. "How come he gets all his bad habits from me?"

"Rotten genes," Lisa responded cheerfully. "Now come on, Jeff, and leave Cally alone. And stop making up stories about flowers in bathtubs." She threw a curious glance at the potted flowers and hanging baskets in the bedroom, then headed for the door.

Mike turned to follow his sister, giving Cally a raised eyebrow over his shoulder. "About those flowers in the bathtub," Cally heard him say to Lisa as they started up the hall.

"What?!" came Lisa's explosive reaction a second later.

"I think she just saw the bathtub," Cally said to Jeff.

"I want to look at the flowers again," Jeff cried, running from the room.

Cally suppressed a laugh as she flung back the covers and grabbed her dress from the chair. At least Mike had neatly folded it there—it made the bedroom look more respectable.

"Hi, again," Cally said sheepishly as she stood at the bathroom door. All three of them were beside the tub like three tourists examining a historical artifact. Jeff had knelt down beside it and was making engine noises as he piloted one of the roses back and forth. "The whole tub is filled," Lisa murmured in wonder. "I've never seen a tub filled with roses."

"How come you got all the flowers, Uncle Mike?" Jeff asked.

"Because ladies like flowers, Jeff, And if you really like a lady you should do something to make her happy."

Jeff shrugged and went back to his rose boat. "Obviously matters of the heart are of no concern at the ripe old age of five," Lisa said. She glanced at her watch and groaned. "We've really got to get going," she said. "Come on, Jeff. We want to get to Grandma's before dinnertime."

"Okay." He stood up, then backed up with a protest of, "Aw, Mom," as Lisa handed him his cap.

"I know this is an affront to your dignity," she said, "but Grandma will kill me if you get an earache."

Jeff looked to Mike as if for confirmation, and Mike nodded solemnly. "Definitely," he said. "Why, I've seen Grandma froth at the mouth with rage."

"He's kidding me again, isn't he, Mom? What's froth anyway?"

"Never mind," she sighed. "I'll explain in the car." She gave Cally a warm smile and reached out to squeeze her hand. "It was lovely meeting you, Cally. I hope I'll see you again soon."

"That would be nice." Cally said, liking the woman.

"And you," she said sternly, turning to her brother. "Keep giving her flowers. She's too good for you, you know."

"Yes, ma'am," Mike said. "You're great for the ego."

"As if you needed any help in that department," Lisa said. She started for the door, Jeff in hand, and kissed Mike on the cheek. "Take care, love." She hugged Cally and whispered in her ear, "I'll give you a hint on keeping him in line. Give him a cookie if he becomes difficult. Worked every time when he was a kid."

Cally laughed. "It may require a bit more now."

Lisa eyed her brother, then looked back at Cally. "Naw."

"I really like her," Cally said when Mike had shut the door.

"She's not so bad for a big sister," he allowed with a grin.

"Did I look all right?" Cally demanded, worried. She touched her hair. "Oh no, I forgot to comb it. I must look like a hillbilly. Was it obvious we'd slept together last night? No, don't answer that. Of course it was obvious. And all those flowers. Lisa must think I'm crazy."

"Shhh," he said, laughing as he put his finger to her lips. "You look absolutely ravishing. You'd look ravishing if you were bald. In fact, it's a good thing your face is so gorgeous."

"Why?" she asked, his flattery bathing her in sunny warmth.

"Because your feet are strictly run-of-the-mill."

Cally glanced down and raised her eyes to him in consternation. "Why didn't you tell me I forgot my shoes?" she cried. "You let me walk around here barefoot in front of Lisa."

"I have it on good authority that Lisa often goes barefoot herself."

She gave him a playful poke to the shoulder with her

fist. "Your sister told me how to handle you, chump."

"And how was that?" The way his mouth was quirking in a lazy smile was making her spine prickle in anticipation of his touch.

"Cookies. She said it worked every time. So don't mess with me."

"You want to try them now?" he asked softly, a decidedly wicked gleam in his eyes.

She pretended to consider, then shook her head. "No. Go ahead and mess with me."

"You got it," he said, scooping her up into his arms. "We can talk cookies later." She nuzzled her face to his neck as he strode to the bedroom with her held tightly against his chest. She touched the pounding pulse at the base of his throat, feeling her own heart surge in answer.

He laid her down on the bed and pressed his mouth to her neck. Without words they began to pleasure each other with their hands and lips, seeking out those most sensitive nerves with intimate knowledge.

The phone shattered the enveloping silence of the room, and Mike cursed softly as he answered it. It was a business call, and Cally lay there watching the change that had washed over him. His voice became brusque as he took command of the situation, cajoling as he convinced the customer it would take a couple of days to get a drill there. With disarming persuasion he got the price he wanted and then hung up. "I'm going to have to go out and supervise that job in a few days," he said, nuzzling her ear. "It's a tricky one. I ought to be gone about a week, but you can stay here, honey. We'll go see some more of the city when I get back."

Her fledgling protests dimmed under his expert touch, and she lay back, losing herself to the moment. Just before she abandoned all reserve to his embrace, she had a fleeting image of him leaving her for each successive job. At best she would have him half the time. *Then take the best,* her pounding heart urged.

She had been in St. Louis four days, and it seemed each succeeding day brought someone new to the door or telephone to chip away what time she and Mike had together. He was leaving tomorrow morning for the new job. He'd take her with him, he said, but work was work and besides, it was a small town with a rinky-dink motel, and he didn't want her locked up there like a pet mouse. *And what am I here?* she wanted to ask.

He was in the bedroom, drinking an imported beer while he took another of the endless phone calls. It seemed that everyone had suddenly discovered that he was home and available.

Cally lay back on the couch in the striped T-shirt dress she'd put on earlier when she and Mike had planned to go out for a late dinner. She kicked off her sandals and watched the TV screen where the tape she and Mike had made glowed with stark clarity. The volume was down, but she could just make out their voices. In her role as Minnie Mouse, she was asking him what he thought of her tail. He nibbled on her ear as he answered, and Cally watched the screen in dry-mouthed fascination. "Ah, my innocent," he said. "If I were to answer that right now, I'd have a blue movie on my hands." On the screen he got up and advanced toward the camera. A second later the tape went blank.

Cally heard him hang up the phone, and she got up to turn off the TV and video machine. She glanced down the hall to the bedroom and saw him sitting on the bed. He hadn't put on his shirt yet, and she found herself staring at the taut muscles of his arms and chest, her fingers curling into her palm as she thought of how those arms responded to her touch.

He glanced up and saw her watching. Smiling ruefully, he walked into the living room, stopping before her to rub his neck. "You must be starved," he said, reaching out to massage her shoulders.

"Not really. Why don't I just mix up some omelets for us here?"

"That sounds good. Listen, honey, I've got some bad news." She held her breath as his eyes moved restlessly over her face, settling with obvious regret on her mouth. "I've got to leave tonight for that new job. Happy's on his way down to the site with the drill, and I've got to meet him there. There's rain in the forecast, and we want to get the drill set up before it all turns to mud." She didn't speak, and he added softly, "I'm sorry."

"It's always going to be like this, isn't it," she said. It wasn't a question. "There's always going to be another job somewhere far away from me. Another good-bye, another door closing."

"Cally." He reached for her hair, but she backed away, seeing his jaw tighten. "I don't want it this way," he said. "If I had my choice I'd stay here with you."

"And what'll I do while you're away?" she asked softly. "I think I'll go talk to my hogs and cattle in Prairie Junction."

"Why can't you stay here in St. Louis?"

"But you're not here," she said quietly. "Isn't that the whole point? I'm a farmer, Mike. I can't just leave a note and say, 'Sorry, hogs. The feed's in the fridge.'"

"Sell the damn farm and marry me," he said, slamming his fist on the top of the couch. His eyes were blue fire, searing in their intensity.

"And what'll I do here while my husband's gone?" she retorted, hating herself but unable to control a sudden wash of anger. "Start a little vegetable garden in the lobby?"

"Be reasonable, Cally." His voice was low and controlled, but she sensed that the steel thread of his patience was about to snap like a cable drawn too taut. "We can work this out."

"By phone?" she snapped.

"We can work it out now. I'm not leaving with you feeling like this."

She heard the hard ring of stubbornness in his voice, and she knew she was incapable of working this problem through now. "Please don't change your plans." she said. "I'm leaving."

"You can't drive home tonight," he protested. "It's too late. I don't want you out on those country roads alone at this hour."

"I'm not driving," she said emphatically. "The truck's yours anyway. I'm leaving it here. I'll take the bus."

He followed her into the den, where she threw her clothes into her suitcase, patently ignoring his angry arguments that what she was doing was foolhardy.

Stubbornness was a wild vetch that entangled them tighter the more they argued. He was still acerbically accusing her of running out on their future as she opened the door and carried her suitcase to the elevator. She heard him call after her as the elevator door closed, and she squeezed her eyes shut to block out his image, which was etched in acid on her brain.

He didn't follow her, and when she climbed into the cab in front of the building, she forced herself not to look up at the fifteenth floor. She didn't want to catch even a glimpse of the man who had asked her to marry him. She'd seen what lay ahead for them, in St. Louis. And she didn't want it.

Chapter Ten

CALLY STOPPED WORKING on the drill long enough to watch a car stop by the side of the road. The purple-pink rays of the setting sun glinted off the windshield. A stooped man with a thatch of white hair got out laboriously and began tacking a notice to the telephone pole. He raised his hammer to Cally before he got back in the car, and she waved. Albert Jones had served as a county fair committeeman for more years than she could count. When she was just a little girl entering her cookies and aprons, he had been one of the cattle judges.

This was the last day of June, so the fair was only a month away. Not that she was keeping track of time. The passage of the summer was of no importance to her. Nor did it matter that it was four weeks, three days, and fourteen hours since she'd left Mike in St. Louis. And in that time she hadn't heard a word from him. Mike's men had finished the hole on John's property and drilled one on her farm, both dry, and then they had gone to St. Louis to work on another job for a while.

Every time a red pickup roared down the road, Cally's heart leaped to her throat, but it was invariably a plain truck, no Donovan name on the side. Not that it mattered, of course.

She reiterated this in a loud voice every morning to the English iris that bloomed in lavender, purple, and white profusion by the road.

The daffodils lining the driveway had long since died and disappeared, and Cally couldn't say she was sorry. The more she thought about it the more the daffodils struck her as Pollyanna flowers—poking up above the ground with bright, cheerful faces before winter was even over. She had grown sick of optimists. English iris was a much more realistic flower. It waited until late June to bloom, choosing the most pleasant weather to appear. Now, she liked English iris. It didn't take risks.

Since she'd grown accustomed to conversing with the daffodils—no matter how one-sided that was—she continued these chats with the iris, shouting above the noise of the churn drill's engine.

"Cross your fingers," she shouted at the iris. "Or your petals, whatever. I'm at the bottom of the last pay zone, and I want to see some oil." She stepped to the back of the drill and threw the gear lever. The clattering engine quieted to a rumbling idle, and the rocking of the drill rig settled down to a docile shudder. She raised the bail bucket out of the hole. Securing her footing on the slick grass, she grasped the bucket and swung it to the hole for the cuttings. Cally emptied the bucket and quickly ran a practiced eye over the pieces of rock and dirt mixed with the water. There was no sign of oil, none at all.

"So you see," she shouted at the iris as she climbed back onto the drill rig, "we have just drilled through the last of the pay zones, the Trenton lime. For those of you iris who are among the uninitiated, pay zones are layers where oil might be found, and we have just exhausted them all." The engine shut off as she turned the switch, and Cally's voice echoed in the still air. She cleared her throat and went on in a calm, lower voice. "This is technically a dry hole, which means I've wasted the better part of seven weeks, not to mention several major muscle groups, and all I have to show for it is a seven-hundred-foot hole in the ground." She stepped down from the rig and slowly took off her heavy gloves. "At least you're not a bunch of know-it-alls like those daffodils," she commented glumly. "Always gossiping behind my back." She tossed the gloves on the back of the rig and started for the house. "And now," she said, pulling herself up straight with great dignity, "I will go fix myself a perfectly awful dinner from the pitiful remnants in the fridge."

She managed to cull an almost-empty jar of peanut butter and a few fresh lettuce leaves from the refrigerator. She'd started a tiny vegetable garden behind the house, and the lettuce was a pale green, young and crisp. There were crackers in the cupboard and a bottle of French dressing. She put on a kettle of hot water and put together a small salad and a plate of peanut butter crackers. When the water boiled, she brewed a pot of chamomile tea in the pot Mike had given her.

The prospect of eating another meal alone was not very appealing. She turned on the radio that sat on the kitchen counter and twisted the dial until she found some quiet piano music. Then she sat at the table with her meager supper and her silverware, and her nicely folded napkin. "This is definitely depressing," she muttered as the radio began a soft rendition of "The Way We Were." She stood up and picked up her peperomia plant from the kitchen window and set it on the table opposite her. She fished out a fertilizer stake from the box under the kitchen sink and poked it into the dirt around the plant. "So nice you could join me for dinner," she said formally, sitting down again. "How did your day go?"

She shook her head. This just wasn't going to work. She stood up and rummaged in the refrigerator again and pulled out a half-full bottle of Japanese plum wine with a flourish. "Conversational lubricant," she said to the peperomia as she sat down. She poured a liberal amount of the wine into her cup of tea and stirred it. "This is good," she said to the plant. "You don't know what you're missing."

By the end of her meal she'd finished off the bottle and was in the process of telling the peperomia about her worry that the iris was becoming too clannish when she heard a noise outside. She stood up to check and swayed as her head pounded. "Is it warm in here, or is it just me?" she asked the peperomia.

She turned on the back-porch light and leaned against

the door, her nose pressed against the glass as she peered out into the gathering dusk. A truck had stopped in the driveway, and Cally squinted, trying to make out whose it was. She cupped her hands around her eyes to see better, a spark leaping from her brain to her heart as she recognized the two men striding toward the house, suitcases in hand.

She was grinning foolishly, still pressed against the glass like a kid looking in the candy-store window. Mike stopped at the door, stared back at her. He seemed to fade into a rising mist, and it dawned on Cally that her breath was fogging the glass.

She stepped back and opened the door. Mike trooped in, followed by Happy. "Well, here we are again," Happy said brightly. "Guess you thought you'd seen the last of us, huh? No such luck. We're opening up the drilling again. We'll start here and then move to the Masters place."

"Hi, Happy," she said, still grinning broadly.

Mike set down his suitcase and said, "We brought back the new truck. And this time make sure you keep it. I haven't gotten a decent night's sleep since you left St. Louis thinking about you driving around in that metal time bomb."

"That wasn't the only reason he couldn't sleep," Happy muttered in a low grumble, and Mike turned to glare at him. "Guess I'll unpack," Happy said, ambling toward the stairs with his suitcase.

Cally and Mike stared at each other. She rocked back on her heels, taking in the way he looked—clean, close-fitting jeans, a light blue cotton shirt that intensified the blue sparks in his eyes, and his dark hair lightly rumpled. He ran his hand through it and she followed the movement, feeling a knot of warmth uncoil in her stomach. She swayed slightly and reached for the counter to steady herself. She caught a glimpse of herself in the toaster, and it was like looking in a funhouse mirror: she hadn't combed her hair or washed her face when she came in from drilling. Tangles of black hair circled her face in wild abandon, and her nose was still smudged with flecks of dirt from her day's work. Her cheeks looked like they belonged on a chipmunk in the distorted toaster reflection. She shook her head as Mike moved toward her. He was frowning, and his jaw was set in a hard line.

"What is going on with you?" he demanded, stopping inches from her. "We've got to talk, Cally. It's time we settled things."

"Shhh," she said in an exaggerated hiss, holding her finger to her lips. "We're not alone." She nodded her head to the direction of the peperomia. "I was having dinner with a friend."

Mike's dark brows knitted together, and he followed her gaze with a slightly confused look. "A houseplant?" he said dubiously.

"A little green friend," she said giving him a lopsided grin.

Mike scrutinized her through narrowed eyes. "You're tipsy," he said, his voice rising. He clamped his hands down on her shoulders and guided her to a kitchen chair. "Sit," he ordered. He picked up the empty wine bottle and shook it experimentally. "Was this full?" he asked incredulously.

She sat back against the chair, feeling incredibly giddy. "At one time." She exploded in giggles. "But I think my friend here was nipping while I was gone. Bottle was only half full tonight." She doubled over in a fresh spurt of giggles. "A potted peperomia."

Mike groaned. "Lady, the peperomia isn't the only thing that's potted around here. Come on. Let's get some fresh air."

He pulled her to her feet, then stood behind her, his hands on her shoulders as he maneuvered her toward the door. Cally carefully planted one foot in front of the other, tottering when the cool evening air hit her face. "So what's the diagnosis, Doc?" she said as he seated her on the porch swing, then sat down beside her. His arm steadied her shoulders as he pulled her over to lean on him.

"For you it's acute tipsiness. For me it's frustration."

She looked up at him, mesmerized by the silvering of his eyes in the dim light. "Frustration?"

He nodded. "I've been trying for the last month to get away so I could settle things with you. A whole month. I finally get here, ready to have it out with you, and you, dear lady, happen to be fried out of your gourd."

Cally giggled and kicked her feet, moving the swing back and forth. "Me and my peperomia," she said. "Hope you don't have anything to settle with it."

"No," he said dryly. "My business is with you."

The swing's motion was making her a little seasick, so she braked with her feet. "What do you want to talk about?"

"Fools and kings," he said softly, giving her the first hint of a smile since he'd walked into her kitchen. "And drills and farms."

"Ah ha!" she cried, holding up one finger in reproof. "You just want me to sell the farm. Hey, this is like one of those old melodramas. The mean banker tries to force the beautiful damsel to marry him or he'll foreclose on her family's farm." There, she'd gone and said the word— marry. It was amazing what a little wine—all right, a lot— could do to your tongue.

There was a moment of silence between them that seemed to stretch into eternity. Cally scuffed her shoe against the porch floor, her eyes lowering. She could feel Mike watching her.

"The villainous banker never gets the girl," he reminded her softly.

"That's right," she said with false brightness. "The hero shows up in time to save her and the farm."

"Always a happy ending." The way he said it, with a tiny thread of cynicism, sobered her more than the evening air could. He'd told her once about choices, and she sensed a choice looming ahead of her, a choice she didn't know if she could make.

"Always a hero," she murmured in reply. "A good guy in a white hat." The chirping chorus of crickets was her only answer.

They sat that way another half hour, and Cally fought the urge to lean her head on Mike's shoulder. No matter how unintentionally she had uttered the word *marry*, it had still been a subtle invitation for him to tell her how he felt about her now that they'd been apart.

Why had he come back looking like he was about to spit the proverbial nails? Sins of omission. The fact that he ignored her shy hint was an icy ramrod that kept her spine stiff. She wouldn't ask him to care for her, either verbally or by putting her head on his shoulder. Sometimes the simplest acts were the most difficult. And sometimes the tough ones came too easily—had his proposal in St. Louis been only a ploy to keep her there?

"Are you feeling better?" he asked, his fingers on her shoulder, turning her slightly toward him.

"Better isn't exactly the operative word," she said quietly, "but things aren't as fuzzy as they were."

"Good." He drew her to her feet and put his hand on her waist. "Why don't you go on to bed? We'll talk in the morning."

"Sure." She wouldn't look at him as he opened the kitchen door for her and followed her in. Her teapot, salad bowl, and the empty wine bottle sat on the table like toy soldiers from a child's mock battle. Resolutely she resisted the urge to clean up and started for the stairs instead. She was too dispirited to face dirty dishes tonight.

"Good night, Cally," he said from behind her.

She gave him a tired answer and kept walking, not looking back.

She was up at dawn the next morning, noticing as she came into the kitchen that he'd washed her dinner plates. She glanced at the teapot he'd put back in its place on the shelf and tightened her lips. Grabbing her work gloves from the top of the refrigerator, she went outside, closing the door quietly behind her. Her head felt mushy, and she absently rubbed her forehead.

She began to warm up and perspire as she prepared to move the Bucyrus Erie off the site. She was massaging her arms after working on the first guy wire when a voice behind her made her jump.

"You left without breakfast."

She spun around and encountered Mike's penetrating gaze. Her face was unguarded, and she quickly lowered her head. "I wasn't very hungry."

"Seems to me you were awfully anxious to avoid me this morning. I was just getting up as you hurried out of the house. Kind of early."

"I had things to do," she said impatiently.

Mike's hand caught her chin and lifted her face. "Looks like you're finished here," he said, nodding toward the rig. "What's the rush?"

She pulled away from his grasp and glared at him, hands on hips. "I want to get set up on a new site."

"Got a permit for a new hole?"

She nodded, taking note of the easy way he stood regarding her, his thumbs hooked in his belt. He had the damnedest way of disrupting her train of thought just by standing there looking at her with a challenging lift of one brow.

"This one's dry, isn't it?" he demanded. Without waiting for her answer he said, "And that explains your little fling with the wine bottle last night."

"It doesn't matter," she said stubbornly. "I'll start a new hole."

Mike shook his head impatiently. "Cally, what is this obsession you have with driving yourself to exhaustion? There's no need for you to waste your time drilling with the Bucyrus Erie. Happy and I can do a hole in two days with the rotary drill."

"I don't really know," she said honestly, her voice dropping. "I just have to try."

Mike half-turned away from her and tilted his head back, closing his eyes. When he swung back to her, his gaze was as piercing and direct as a hot blue streak of electricity. Her skin prickled with heat. "Then we'd better get to work," he said.

"What?" She stared in bewilderment as he began rolling up his sleeves.

He pulled a pair of gloves from his pocket. "I've just become your drilling partner."

"You've got your own work to do," she protested.

"Happy and the boys can handle it. Besides, I'm only a shout away if they need something." He began loosening the guy wires stabilizing the derrick. "Come on, lady," he said over his shoulder. "Let's get busy, or I might think up some better things to do with our time."

She could think of better things, too, and as his shoulders strained against the fabric of his shirt she felt an anticipatory shiver.

When the guy wires had been removed, Mike began lowering the derrick to a horizontal position above the cab. The day was heating up, and he wiped his brow with his shirt sleeve. Together they raised the jacks used to level the rig.

He opened the door for her to climb in, then touched her on the arm. "Cally," he said softly, "what happens if you don't find oil?"

She met his questioning gaze without wavering. "I have to," she said simply. She saw something flicker over his face—indecision? regret?—before he masked it. "Then we'd better start drilling," he said, closing the door.

The new site was behind the feedlot in a cornfield. They had to drive the drill rig over the lower part of the field to reach it, and Mike darted her a sideways smile. "We're ruining your corn, Mrs. Taylor," he said.

"I'll have to speak to your boss about it," she said with mock severity. "I hear he's a real tough guy."

"He's mellowed considerably, my dear. Fact is, the lady with the Bucyrus Erie has him wrapped around her little finger."

"Hah!" As the rig rolled to a stop she hopped out. "You're about as susceptible to female wiles as this rig is."

He climbed down and stood grinning at her, hands on hips. "I could give you a demonstration right now if you'd like. There's not a soul around."

"Donovan, you're hopeless. Put your libido in neutral, and let's get to work." She turned away from his smile, hiding her own glow of pleasure. It looked like she wouldn't have to talk to the flowers for a while. The poor English iris. They'd have to gossip among themselves.

When she turned around from the back of the rig he was standing right behind her, and she found herself staring at his shirt buttons, growing heady from the warm, musky scent of him. "I guess we ought to set up the derrick," she murmured in a near-whisper.

"Yeah, the derrick."

Neither of them made a move. Cally's fingers ran restlessly to his chest, fanning out and stroking the soft fabric, tingling at the increased tempo of his heartbeat.

His head lowered to hers, blotting out the sun. Her fingers curled against his chest as he pressed her tightly against him, and his mouth took hers with such fierceness that she swayed against him. She didn't want it to ever end, and she pretended she didn't hear the sound of an approaching motor. Apparently Mike didn't care either, because the pressure on her mouth didn't diminish at all. Even after a horn honked, he continued the kiss another full three seconds, breaking it with a muttered oath when the horn honked again. His arms were still around her when he turned to face the intruder.

"Where do you want me to drill today?" Happy demanded from the truck, a broad grin creasing his face as he watched them.

"Anywhere but here," Mike growled, still not relinquishing his hold on Cally. "Try the moon."

"Good idea, boss," Happy said. "But you're in charge of transportation."

"I'll get you to the moon all right," Mike said. Releasing Cally, he turned toward the truck. "Help Tom out. You should be able to finish up that hole today."

Happy tipped his hat and left, and Cally asked, "Do you think there's oil in the hole they're on?"

Mike studied her face before answering. Slowly and deliberately he said, "I don't know. There was a small show of live oil on top of the Silurian layer." He glanced at her face and frowned. "Don't get your hopes up, Cally. You know as well as I do that that doesn't mean there's more oil there."

"But it means there's a chance." She turned back to the rig, humming. It didn't even bother her when she dropped the heavy sledgehammer they used to drive in the pegs holding the guy wires. "Oops," she chirped cheerfully when it missed her toes by inches.

She looked up and saw Mike's eyes on her, but even his pensive stare couldn't shake her mood.

She went back to the house before Mike so she could get lunch started. She was making tuna salad sandwiches when Happy came in to wash up.

"How's it going?" she asked eagerly.

Happy shook his head. "Dry hole. We're gonna pull off the site this afternoon and set up over on John's place. Maybe we'll have better luck there."

"No oil," Cally repeated softly, putting down the bowl of tuna salad.

Happy shook his head, mopping his face with a red bandanna. "John said he'll finance two more holes, so that's one on his land and one on yours. We'll be finished up here in another week, I imagine. But I guess Mike told you all that already."

No, Mike hadn't told her. Happy went upstairs to clean up, and Cally stood staring down at the sink. It would take less than a week to drill two more holes, and then he'd be gone. She could imagine what would happen then—a phone call between jobs, maybe one more visit on a Sunday when he was off. She would stay on the farm doggedly running the Bucyrus Erie. She could picture herself at ninety, beating the side of the rig with her cane as she drilled the hundredth hole in search of oil. Already she was lonely. Slamming the loaf of bread down on the kitchen table, she grabbed her keys and fled the kitchen. Her only thought at the moment was to get away and think. Things were coming unraveled. She saw Mike walking toward the house from the drill site and saw him stop in puzzlement as she jumped in Daffy and ground the motor to life. She gunned the engine and sped down the drive. Without thinking. she turned the truck up the edge of the field, following the path there. Two dry wells in two days. Mike was leaving in a week.

She clenched her teeth and didn't slow down for the ruts, bouncing hard against the spring in the seat. She hit another bump hard and finally slowed down, trying to massage her aching thigh where the spring had poked it. The truck coughed once, slowed, and coughed again. Not now, she groaned to herself. Not now.

But Daffy apparently had little concern for her feelings, because he chose that moment to wheeze to a stop. She pounded the steering wheel in frustration and tried to restart the engine. But the truck had lost all consciousness. "Senile piece of metal," she mumbled, climbing down and looking around.

Daffy's demise couldn't have been more poorly timed. She was at the spot where she and Mike had planned a picnic a few weeks ago. The gnarled hazelnut tree stood sentry by the stream, an impassive observer. She stooped and pulled a strand of thick grass and absently chewed on it as she walked toward the stream. It reminded her of the stream on Mike's property, and she leaned against the hazelnut tree, closing her eyes.

An approaching motor drew her attention, and she turned around as Mike pulled to a stop in the new yellow truck. She turned her back on him, her arms crossed, shoulders rigid.

She heard the door slam, heard his deliberate footsteps behind her. It was a moment before he spoke. "Was this a scheduled stop?"

She shook her head. "The damn truck died."

"I'm sorry there wasn't any oil, Cally," he said softly.

Tears filled her eyes and she angrily brushed at them with her arm, wishing he'd leave her alone with her self-pity. "I don't want to talk now," she said stiffly. "Please go away, Mike."

"I can't leave you like this," he said. "I can't stand to see you hurting, Cally." His hand touched her hair, and Cally jumped away, determined not to accept his comfort. She started to run toward the stream, just wanting to be alone.

"Cally!" He was running after her, and she increased her speed. It wasn't Mike she was trying to escape; it was her own helplessness. She stumbled down the bank of the stream, startling a flock of sparrows that exploded into the air in panic. She leaped from one rock to the next to reach the opposite bank. She was almost there when she slipped on the last moss-covered rock as her shoe slid sideways. Her arms flailed the air and she tilted over, falling into the water. Her knees hit first and then her hands as she tumbled forward. She propped herself up on one hand and wiped her face with her other sleeve, then heaved a small rock at the shore in frustration.

She turned to see Mike wading in after her, a grim expression on his face. "Are you hurt?" he asked, helping her up.

Her knees and palms stung where they'd landed on the pebbles at the bottom of the stream, but she shook her head. "Just a flesh wound," she muttered bitterly.

She slipped again as she tried to get back up the bank, and Mike scooped her up, carrying her the rest of the way.

At contact with his hard body she realized why she had run from him. It wasn't the dry oil wells, and it wasn't the farm. It was Mike. She was in love with him.

With a little sigh she pressed her head against his neck. He sat down on the grass with her on his lap and stroked her hair. "I'm sorry, Cally," he murmured against her hair. "So sorry, baby." She clenched her hands against his shirt, abandoning herself to the sheer pleasure of his touch. "We could dry your clothes in the sun," he said, nuzzling her ear. There was a pause before he added hopefully, "Of course that would necessitate your taking them off."

"I think that could be arranged," she murmured, smiling against his shoulder.

She lifted her head to meet his lips as he began tugging off her T-shirt, his fingers lingering to mount a slow, sensual assault on her breasts. She arched her back and her hair fell over the curve of his arm.

"Cally," he groaned, pulling her shirt over her head and laying it aside. "Those weeks after you left St. Louis were hell." He bent his leg to support her back and began to suck and nibble her breasts, his hand straying down her hip. *He'll be gone in a week,* a voice nagged in her head. But it didn't matter at the moment. She loved him.

His mouth met hers in a hungry encounter that robbed her of any vestiges of reserve. His tongue drove into her as his hands on her bare shoulders drew her even closer. He was a whirlpool of flames, the heat dragging her deeper into desire. Cally twined her fingers in his hair, luxuriating in the remembered texture.

His mouth still fastened to hers, he peeled off his own shirt and then unfastened her jeans. She started to stand up to remove them, but Mike held her to him. "Don't move," he whispered hoarsely. "I don't want to let you go." He pulled off her shoes and socks, then lifted her slightly and pulled off the jeans. Mike pressed her tightly to him again, as though afraid the breeze would carry her away from him like an airborne dandelion seed.

She traced his collarbone with her tongue, and his fingers responded with a tantalizing exploration down her spine and over her hips. "If I could figure out some way of getting my own pants off without moving you, I'd be a genius," he said breathlessly, his eyes glowing with unabashed desire as he looked down at her.

"There must be something about this in the sex manuals," she whispered, trailing her finger down his chest.

"This is better than any manual, love. You ought to come with a label—*Warning: Addictive.*" He lifted her to her knees and knelt before her, kissing the sensitive valley between her breasts as he undid his pants. He slipped them to his knees, then sat back and pulled them off. Grinning at her wickedly, he hooked one finger in the lace of her underpants and tugged them down with excruciating slowness. When he had them at her knees he ran his hands back up her thighs, eliciting a low moan from her. His fingers brushed over her most sensitive areas, touching and igniting fires deep inside her. She was swaying as he pulled her over on top of him. As her mouth met his, she dimly noted that his cheekbones were flushed, and it made her giddy to know she had that effect on him. She was sure her own passion shone through her eyes, and she made no effort to hide it. She wanted him, and she wanted him to know it. She gloried in the feel of his lean, taut body beneath her and the sweet smell of summer grass around them. "Kiss me again, honey," he whispered as he nuzzled her throat, "and let's see if we can write a new chapter for those manuals."

She bent her head to his again, and he caught her lower lip in his teeth, teasing it with tiny bites. He twisted a piece of her hair around his finger, then rolled them both over so he was leaning over her. "I love you, Cally," he murmured. "My sweet, beautiful lady. Let me love you."

"I love you, too," she whispered softly. "Say it again, Mike."

"I love you . . . love you," he said raggedly, spreading her thighs with his knee. The hair on his legs rasped against her own flesh as he raised her hips to meet his. Her breath caught in her throat as the pressure built, and the pleasure became overpoweringly sweet. She gasped his name.

Her throbbing pulse became the only sound she could hear, like the roar of a waterfall as she was swept downstream. The roar grew closer, and then she was swept over the edge, her heart pounding madly.

* * *

The warm sun dried the film of perspiration on her back as she lay cradled in his arms, their legs entwined. "Did anyone ever tell you you're beautiful?" he said lazily, kissing her nose.

"I recall you mentioning it once," she said, leaning back to look at him fondly.

"Dearest lady, you're getting vain." He pulled her head back to his and kissed her.

"I hope not too vain for old Love-'Em-And-Leave-'Em Donovan," she said lightly, rolling over to get her T-shirt. She felt his eyes on her as she dressed. "Am I supposed to be leaving you?" he asked.

She glanced at him from under her eyelashes and saw him lying on his back, completely at ease, his arms crossed under his head. "I hear you'll finish drilling in about a week."

"Cally, I'm not walking out of your life." He hadn't moved. His voice hadn't changed. But there was an undercurrent that riveted her attention.

"But you *are* leaving?" Slowly she tucked in her T-shirt as he stood up and reached for his clothes. He pulled on his jeans before answering.

He'll stay here with you, her heart cried. *He loves you.*

"We've got some work in southern Missouri," he said quietly. "Water wells."

"Do you have to go?" She hated herself for asking the minute the words left her mouth. The last thing she'd do would be to beg him to stay. She'd tried that once, hadn't she? Not even for Mike Donovan's love would she forget her pride again. "Never mind," she said "I know the answer."

"I have to go, Cally, I can't run a drilling company from Prairie Junction when most of my work is in southern Missouri." He zipped his pants and straightened. "Come with me, Cally. Marry me."

Her hands stilled their nervous toying with her shirt, tucking and retucking it. "Marry you?" Her voice was barely a whisper.

"In case you forgot, I asked once in St. Louis. It's hardly a surprise question, is it?"

She shook her head. "I suppose not. I don't know. And

you practically ordered me to marry you in St. Louis. It wasn't really a question." Her lonely heart began kicking her with impatient irritation. What was the matter with her? She loved him. He loved her. The logical conclusion was marriage, wasn't it? This was a simple equation, and she'd gotten an A in algebra.

"What's wrong, Cally? Is it the farm?" His voice was sharp, probing her subconscious like a white-hot needle.

She stared at the ground, her mind whirling with the energy of a tornado. "I suppose so," she said.

"Let it go. Cally. Let the past end. You can't go on hanging on to it forever." His voice was searing, and if he had touched her with his breath she would have burned.

"I'm trying."

"Are you, Cally?" The sharpness of his indictment made her take a defensive step backward. "Or are you hanging on to it because you're afraid to let go?"

Cally's chin came up defiantly. "Let it go for what, Mike? A life with a man who will be gone most of the time, working in out-of-the-way back roads for days, weeks, at a time? I told you once—I can't play out my days in your apartment watching the traffic."

"Then what, Cally? What do you want? Tell me."

"I want you."

"Then we can work out the rest of it. Trust me."

She wanted to believe that it would all turn out right, that somehow he'd make it work, and looking at him standing there in his jeans, soft grass cushioning his bare feet, his chest hard and tanned, she wanted to believe. "All right," she said softly. "We'll work it out."

He crossed to her soundlessly and took her in his arms, an act of possession for both of them. He had come into her life with the force of a March wind ruffling everything in its path, but when she was in his arms like this the force and power of Mike Donovan was the gentlest, most wonderful thing she'd ever known. "Oh, Donovan," she sighed. "You could charm the pants off my maiden aunt."

"Forget your maiden aunt," he whispered in her ear. "I'm addicted to those silky little lace numbers you wear."

"Remind me to give you a souvenir pair," she said wryly, riffling her hand through his hair.

"Come on, lady," he said, giving her an affectionate pat on the behind. "I might just take you up on that. Now let's go get some lunch. All this lewd talk has gotten my appetite up."

"Among other things," she laughed, glancing pointedly at his jeans. She raced to the truck with Mike in pursuit, threatening to do vile things to her body if he caught her. She tossed her shoes on the floor and teased him by locking his door.

They left Daffy sitting forlornly as they headed back to the house together, and Cally glanced over her shoulder at the abandoned truck, feeling a pang of remorse. There was always pain in leaving something old and comfortable behind, no matter how worn out it was.

Mike cooked Chinese food for dinner later that night. It was his famous Peking duck, he claimed, though it had turned out to be roast chicken with a plum sauce that Mike insisted was an old family recipe. One look at the empty plum-jelly jar on the counter and Cally figured she knew that recipe.

She was washing dishes after dinner when she stepped on a piece of onion Mike had dropped while preparing dinner. Remembering she'd left her shoes in the truck— she went barefoot more often than not in the summer—she thought she'd better retrieve them before she stepped on any more of Mike's culinary accidents.

Dew was beginning to gather on the grass, and her feet were cool and damp when she opened the truck door. She picked up her shoes and sat down on the seat to put them on. A folder of Mike's papers was balanced precariously on the dashboard, and she pushed it back. She started to leave the truck, then sat back down as it registered what the top of the protruding piece of paper said. *Geology Report. Taylor-Masters Sites.*

She reached for the folder and pulled out the report, sitting back to read it. Mike had apparently sent the state some rock samples from the wells he'd already drilled on her property and John's.

She frowned as she read the word *negative* after several sample numbers. Her heart was pounding, and foreboding closed in like the gathering dusk. Hurriedly she skipped to the end of the report. *Prospects negative*. That was the notation in Mike's handwriting. He knew there was no hope of finding oil. He knew. And yet he'd come back anyway to feed her empty promises. She'd bought the same bag of smoke Dan had.

She threw the papers back on the dashboard before her anger made her rip them apart. Slamming the door, she ran for the house.

Her hands were shaking as she continued washing dishes. Happy had gone out for a walk and Mike was upstairs showering.

"Want some help?"

Her back stiffened into steely resistance at the sound of his voice. In the darkened window over the sink she could see his reflection, mirrored three hazy times. She wasn't sure which one was really Mike Donovan, and she was less sure that she'd recognize the real man if she turned around.

"I think you've helped enough," she said, breaking a soap bubble in the pan with her finger.

"What's that supposed to mean?" The wariness in his voice matched her own, and she felt the air between them grow heavy with tension.

She turned slowly, wiping her hands on the dish towel, then tossed it on the counter. "It means I read the geology report."

His voice reverberated in the thick air, making ripples the way a stone invades a pond. "Cally, listen to me."

"No." The finality of the word stunned even her. "No, I won't listen to any other lies."

"I never lied to you." Time spun down to a crawl, and the vividness of the moment washed over her. His dark hair was damp from the shower, and she helplessly remembered the day he'd come to see her in the rain, and the way the droplets clung to him.

He'd changed into a black polo shirt and beige slacks, and he looked like he should be holding a glass of wine as he admired a costly painting in his fancy living room. He didn't belong in her kitchen. He didn't belong in her life.

"There are lots of ways of lying," she said.

The silence was measured by the sound of the clock.

Night seemed to descend like a curtain with each tick. "There's oil on this land, Cally. I'm sure of it. It's just a matter of time."

"Don't," she said brokenly. "I don't want to hear any more sweet promises. They're starting to taste very bitter. Just leave."

"Is that the answer?" he demanded. "Throwing me out to solve all your problems?"

"It's the best answer I've got right now," she said, fighting to retain her composure. "Please leave tomorrow morning. You can keep drilling for John if you want, but I don't want you here."

"That's very civilized of you," he said coldly, "but I'll make it easy on you. I'll leave right now. And before you congratulate yourself on your self-righteousness, let me tell you one thing. John Masters saw the geology report, and he made the decision to continue drilling. He pays us, Cally, not you. So what John says goes. I may be guilty of not hitting you in the face with the cold, hard truth, but I never took advantage of you."

"Yes you did," she said angrily, fighting back against the urge to feel his arms holding her. Only a few words, a few steps and he would embrace and comfort her. And she'd believe him all over again. "You took advantage of me when you said you loved me."

"That's the irony," he said with a hollow laugh. "I do love you. Though sometimes I wonder why." Before his words sank in, he had turned and left the room. Cally knew he was going to pack his things, and she turned back to the dishes, feeling the need to keep her hands busy. But it was no good. She was washing the teapot when she heard a sound from upstairs, a drawer slamming, and when she turned to glance at the stairs, the teapot slipped from her soapy hands and crashed to the floor. It broke into a hundred pieces before she even realized she'd dropped it. Her hand flew to her mouth and then to her eyes as she bit back tears of anger and loss. She couldn't be hurting more if each piece of jagged china had lodged in her heart.

Using a broom and dust pan from the closet, she swept up the pieces and dumped them into the trash basket. The act of cleaning up the floor put a stamp of finality on her insistence that Mike move out, and she turned to leave the kitchen. It was better that she didn't watch him go. She went to the hogpen and ran water from the hose into the water trough while the hogs jockeyed for position and snorted. Above the noise of the hogs she heard the screen door slam, and the sharp bang made her quicken her movements to cover up the sound of his leaving. The truck door shut, that metallic clang carrying across the summer air to the hog lot. She never heard the engine start, though her muscles ached with the tension of anticipating it.

When she finally walked back from the hog lot the truck was still parked in the driveway, and she glanced nervously toward the house. She was too weary to argue with him tonight. He wasn't in the kitchen when she went in, and she watched the stairs warily, tensing when she heard a noise. Happy stepped from his room and looked down at her. "You seen Mike?" he asked, rubbing his stubbly chin with a towel.

Cally stared past him toward Mike's empty room. "I asked him to leave," she said in a low voice.

Happy's hand stopped in mid-motion. "What did he do, Cally? I'll straighten him out."

She half-smiled at the outraged tone of his voice. She shook her head. "It's nothing, Happy. Don't worry about it. Just get a good night's sleep." She went back to the kitchen, purposely not looking at the trash can, and sat down at the kitchen table. She lowered her head to her hands and waited for the voice of reason in her head to make a caustic comment. But even reason was silent tonight.

Chapter Eleven

CALLY LEFT THE house woodenly the next morning, and the singing of the cardinal in the redbud tree was cacophony to her ears. The air was still heavy with morning dew, and the dampness clung to her like a spider web. She ran her hand through her hair as she glanced warily at the yellow truck in the driveway. The question of where Mike had gone last night nagged at her. It didn't matter, she told herself.

She stopped cold as the truck door creaked. Mike stepped out, obviously stiff. He wasn't looking in her direction, and he stretched slowly, grimacing as he massaged his back. He'd slept in the truck. She felt a pang and sharply reminded herself again that it didn't matter.

She told herself to turn her back on him and walk away, but her brain had apparently shut down, refusing to send any signals to her legs. Feeling idiotic, she stood rooted to the spot.

When Mike glanced in her direction he froze, and for a moment he looked like a man who'd just been hit in the stomach with a baseball bat. Cally might have run to him at that moment, but quickly he wiped the expression from his face.

159

Slowly she turned and started toward the feedlot. He didn't say anything, and she resisted the desire to look over her shoulder.

The chores drained her that morning, and when she got to the Bucyrus Erie she felt as though she'd already put in a full day's work. The temptation was to return to the house, and she sat down on a cement block near the rig and just stared at the ground. She plucked a dandelion and rubbed it against her finger. But the coarse texture reminded her of the times she'd run her fingers through Mike's hair, and she threw the weed on the ground, grinding it with her foot.

Setting the jacks on the front and back of the rig took an inordinate amount of time, and when the bubble finally centered to the level, she sank down on the ground in relief. Had the earth's gravity increased overnight? Her limbs felt leaden.

It took her twice as long to raise the derrick and start positioning the guy wires, and when she glanced at her watch she saw that most of the morning had passed. She stared out to the east, toward the site where Mike was drilling with his hydraulic rig, and she straightened her spine when she saw the sun dance off the tip of the derrick. She turned back to the Bucyrus Erie and kicked it for spite. Having in all probability permanently dented her toe, she figured she'd indulged in enough self-abuse. Anchoring the guy wires just about depleted her remaining strength, and when she finally put down the sledgehammer she was drenched with perspiration.

She started up the motor on the back of the rig and engaged the levers, throwing the drill into gear. The bit came down on the ground in rhythmic thuds, rocking the rig with its force.

At last she could sit back and rest a moment. Her hair was plastered to her forehead in damp strands, and she tilted her face up toward the breeze, closing her eyes.

"Don't you think you've accomplished whatever it is you set out to prove?" It was Mike's voice carrying over the steady hum of the rig, and she spun toward the sound. He was standing just a few feet away, the cobalt blue of his eyes blazing like chunks of stormy sky. She turned back to the rig, her hands trembling, and pretended to check the gauges.

"I'm not out to prove anything," she retorted.

"Yes you are. You want the world to know that Cally Taylor can run this farm all by herself and put in a full day's work on a drill besides. And she doesn't need anyone or anything. Do you, lady?" The last was delivered in a low, cutting drawl that knifed through her like a falling icicle cutting into a snow drift. Except this was June, and his voice shouldn't make her think of winter.

"I don't need your pretty little dreams," she said in an equally cold voice.

"We all need dreams," he said, his voice just as hard, but the cutting edge was gone. "That's why you're out here drilling today, Cally. That's what keeps you going."

She didn't want to hear about dreams when hers were lying broken on the ground. He moved a step closer, and Cally backed away. The water she'd poured in the hole to keep the bit cool had turned the grass and dirt there to mud, and her shoe slipped. She threw out her arm for balance, but it was a futile gesture as her other foot slid from under her.

Mike's hand closed on her arm and jerked her to him, dragging her against his body. Leaning against his chest breathlessly, she stared up at his face. What she saw there made her runaway pulse throb against her throat. "You're going to get hurt working alone," he said almost angrily, and she found herself trembling because of her proximity to him.

Her voice was shaking when she answered. "And never star in another sex manual," she said in an attempt to defuse his anger.

"Cally." His voice embodied humor, exasperation, and relief all in that one word. He murmured her name again, and she didn't resist when he cradled her head to his chest and kissed her hair. "Didn't you realize that I just wanted to give you something?" he asked softly. "You were so hurt when the well you drilled—and then mine—both came up dry. I couldn't tell you about the geology report." He was rocking her gently back and forth against him. "All you'd accept from me was the teapot. I knew I was in for a hell of a fight when I tried to give you the truck." He laughed softly. "There wasn't anything else I could give you but the dream of finding oil."

"I broke the teapot," she said against his shirt, her voice hoarse. "I dropped it."

"I'll get you a hundred more just like it," he said, rubbing his chin against her hair.

She squeezed her eyes shut, breathing in his closeness, and the image of Mike's leaving leaped out at her. It was so compelling that she pushed away from him slightly. "I'm all right now," she said quietly. "I should get back to work."

"What's wrong?" His eyes searched her face.

"It's better we don't start anything now that we'll break off anyway in a few days." Her hands lingered on his chest, then dropped. She turned away from him to stare at the drill.

"Break it off? What are you talking about?" His hands touched her shoulders, his fingers communicating his growing agitation with tensile strength. "I asked you to marry me, Cally, and I meant it."

"I can't marry you." She focused on the bail bucket as if hypnotizing herself to concentrate only on the words she was saying and not the feel of his sensual fingers sliding to the hollows between her neck and shoulders.

He turned her around, and her concentration fled as she met his gaze, heavy with stormy tension. His thumbs moved to her collarbone, circling it restlessly. "It isn't just the geology report that's bothering you, is it?" he demanded in a husky voice.

"We've been over this," she said wearily, her eyes dropping to his shirt buttons. "Let's just forget it."

"No, I don't want to forget it." His voice was harsh, and she stiffened as his grip tightened. "I'm not waltzing out of your life no matter how hard you push me, lady. You keep pushing, and you'll see just how immovable I can be."

She had no doubt he meant it, but it didn't alter the circumstances or lessen her resolve. Her voice cracked with emotion. "Your idea of staying in my life is a series of hit-and-miss encounters. You'll come and go as you please, expecting me to keep a light in the kitchen window for your infrequent arrivals. And for every arrival there's a departure. Forget it, Donovan. I don't need that kind of pain."

Their eyes met and clashed, smoldering with barely contained anger. Blue and gray, sky and smoke.

"Do you think I enjoy the good-byes?" he asked harshly. "When I'm away from you all I can think about is holding you close to me, burying my face in your neck and making love to you until everything else is blotted out." He took a deep, shaking breath, his eyes roving her face hungrily. "But I can't stay here, Cally. I've told you that."

"Sell the farm," she said bitterly. "That's your answer to everything."

"It's a start, dammit," he exploded, dropping his hands from her shoulders. He hooked his thumbs in his belt and leaned back, tilting his jaw. "If you don't like the St. Louis apartment I'll get something else."

"And what would that change?" she demanded stubbornly. "Instead of saying good-bye in St. Louis we'd say good-bye somewhere else every time you left for another job."

"I won't call it quits," he reiterated calmly and adamantly.

"Leave me be, Mike," she said shakily.

He shook his head. "I'm sorry if I'm hurting you, Cally, but I can't let you go. Not now, and not ever."

"Then at least let me drill in peace. Go away, Mike."

She turned to the rig and pushed the lever to stop the drill, praying he'd just leave without further conversation. She couldn't stand any more good-byes. The lever jammed, and Cally pushed on it, taking out her frustration. Mike's hand closed over hers, and the vibrations running through her weren't from the rig; they were the wild thumping of her heart. She stared down at his hand—bronzed, strong, and capable. Unwilling memories of how that hand felt roaming possessively over her bare flesh made her shiver. Gently he uncurled her fingers from the lever and efficiently unjammed it. "Thank you," she said stiffly over the hum of the engine. She didn't look at him, and after a moment he touched her chin tentatively, turning her toward him. He studied her for a long minute, and a warmth surpassing that of the sun suffused her face.

"Have you eaten anything today?" he asked, frowning.

The question surprised her, and she shook her head in bewilderment.

"I thought as much. You sure take lousy care of yourself. Wait a minute." He strode to the truck and returned with a paper bag. "I packed you some lunch." She took the bag and opened it warily. Inside were a wax-paper–wrapped sandwich, an apple, and some cookies. "Nothing fancy," Mike said. "But it's food. Now sit down and eat." Without waiting for a reply, he moved to the rig and began raising the cable. She stood watching as he emptied the five-gallon barrel of water into the hole and then started the drill again. The drill cable began its rhythmic ascent and descent, rising five feet, then lowering to pound the earth with the bit. *Thud, thud.* She wasn't sure if it was the rig or her pounding pulse shaking the earth where she stood. Slowly she sank to the ground, clutching her lunch, feeling like a child whose independence had been cut short. He turned to glance at her over his shoulder, and it didn't matter what he did, just so he stayed with her. Even if it was only a few more days.

Settling back, she tentatively opened the sandwich and made a face at Mike. "Bologna. Yech!" she mouthed. He laughed and gave his attention back to the rig.

Six days passed—six of the liveliest days Cally had ever known. The corn seemed larger and greener than she'd ever seen it, and it rustled at night like taffeta. The summer air was more sweetly perfumed with flowers, and each blade of grass seemed a miracle in itself. And all because Mike Donovan was beside her every minute. He'd insisted on spending his remaining time on the farm helping her with the Bucyrus Erie, claiming she'd drop the bail bucket on her head if he didn't. The slightest touch of his arm against hers sent an earthquake of sensual tremors through her, and on the second day—after they'd spent the morning bumping into each other—he called "break time" and took her in his arms, kissing her until she thought she'd lose all touch with the earth below her feet. After that, it became a game to them, and one or the other would call break time at least once an hour.

It was all ending today though. Happy and the boys had

finished the last two holes, and both were dry. John Masters had decided to wait until he sold his wheat before paying for any more holes, and the Donovan Drilling Company was moving on to southern Missouri.

Cally stood in the kitchen doorway, holding the door as Happy carried out his suitcase. She let the screen door bang behind her and walked toward the truck where Mike was tying down equipment on the back.

He hopped down and stood looking at her, and for a long moment neither of them said anything. Knowing he was leaving, she'd dressed carefully this morning, and Mike's eyes moved over her slowly and approvingly. She wore a red wraparound skirt with a ruffle at the hem, and a white cotton blouse with a V-neck that was laced with red ribbon. Her long black hair was straight and burnished to a sheen.

"Sure you won't come along?" he asked softly.

She shook her head, straining to keep the smile on her face.

"And you won't keep this truck?" he asked.

"No. I called Harley, and he's going to tow Daffy in and have his brother try to resuscitate him."

Again they fell silent, and Cally could hear the piping voices of the baby wrens in the old wren house in the redbud tree. The air was already sultry, though it was early morning, and she knew that by afternoon waves of heat would be rising from the blacktop road, as tangible as steam.

"Honey, I'm going to miss you," he said in a low voice.

"Me, too."

He glanced wryly at Happy sitting in the truck and gave Cally a chaste peck on the cheek. "Bye, Cally." He started for the driver's side and stopped in mid-stride. Purposefully he walked back to her. "Aw, hell," he grumbled. He pulled her to him, nearly lifting her off the ground with his arms wrapped around her waist. His mouth sought hers with evident greed, and Cally's own desire surged to the surface, her lips claiming his for kiss.

"It's not easy to say good-bye to you," he whispered, his mouth lifting slightly at the corners.

"I don't want to make it easy on you," she said fiercely.

"Then you're succeeding very well," he murmured against her neck. Slowly he straightened, still holding her pressed against him. "See you later, beautiful lady." It seemed to take an effort on his part to release her. He took a step backward and then walked to the truck and climbed in. Cally stood on the grass as he started the engine and backed away quickly. She waved, and Happy waved back, but Mike was watching the drive behind him. At the road, she saw him stop and stare up at her before pulling away quickly. Cally sighed and started for the house. There was a butterfly flitting around the lilac bush by the back door, and she stopped to watch it. It was a monarch, black markings vivid on an orange background. She remembered reading somewhere that monarchs migrated to Mexico for the winter. "Just like a man," she said to the butterfly. "Coming and going. Always saying good-bye." She stalked into the house and slammed the door.

Chapter Twelve

"YES, MRS. COLMAN," Cally said into the phone wearily. "No, it doesn't matter what brand of graham crackers she uses in her piecrust." She peered out the window, making appropriate clucks of agreement as Mrs. Colman went on about Laura's entries in the county fair. Despite the heat, the windows were all shut because of the flies. That was one of the problems with raising hogs. Cally had opened the front door and put an electric fan there. It didn't cool the house, but it stirred the air a bit.

"No," Cally said, "you don't need to enclose a note with Laura's apron. It's not that important to the judges what kind of thread she used for the hem." She stared at the derrick of the Bucyrus Erie that rose in the cornfield. If she got right out there after she hung up she might finish up the hole by evening. She'd taken a break to get the mail and eat some lunch, only to be ensnared by Mrs. Colman's phone call. She glanced at the letter on the table and fingered it carefully. She'd been about to open it when the phone rang.

"All right, Mrs. Colman. Yes, I'll be there when Laura gives her demonstration. No, it doesn't matter what she wears. Okay. Good-bye."

She hung up and slowly turned the letter over in her hand. It was the first letter Mike had written since he'd left almost a month ago. Lying awake during the sultry Illinois nights, she had finally decided she wouldn't hear from him again.

Cally pocketed the letter and started for the door. She'd read it while the rig was running.

She had bailed out the hole just before she came into the house, and now she poured another five gallons of water down the hole and lowered the cable and bit. When the drill was making its usual *ker-chunk* against the slate she sat down on the grass and opened the letter.

> *Hi, Beautiful Lady,*
>   *We finally finished the wells here. Happy says if I don't get back up to Prairie Junction soon he's going to stick me in a crate and ship me there. By the way, I sent you a present.*
>
>   *Love,*
>   *Mike*

She turned the letter over, but that was it. No mention of when he was coming back. In fact, she thought in irritation, he didn't even bother to mention why it took him so long to write. "Donovan," she said between clenched teeth. "Wait until I get my hands on you." She jammed the letter into her pocket and scowled at the rig. "What I ought to do is show up on your doorstep and agree to marry you. Then I could drive you as crazy as you've driven me. I'd have a lifetime to pay you back."

Her imagination took flight. She could call Donna and have the farm sold in a matter of days. She could be in St. Louis right after the county fair was over, and she could start a lifetime with Mike Donovan. Or half a lifetime. Maybe he wouldn't be right there with her all the time, but Mike Donovan half the time had to be far better than what she had now.

With a start she realized she was serious. She wanted to marry him even if it meant these awful separations. Slowly she let her eyes wander around the farm. The fence around the feedlot was sagging in several places again, and it would have to be patched before winter. The wind had loosened shingles on the house, and a windowpane was cracked where a flying branch had hit it early in January. The paint had completely peeled from the house this winter, leaving the boards a uniform faded gray. The shrubs and bushes had all grown without benefit of trimming and looked wild and unkempt.

She could see the end of the driveway from here, and she noticed that weeds had reclaimed the edge of the drive where the daffodils had bloomed. For the first time, the sight of all this neglect didn't hurt her anymore. This was an old farm with an old house, and there were hundreds like it in this part of Illinois. It was time that this place passed to someone who could give it the love and attention it deserved. She felt a momentary pang, but it quickly went away, and she realized that over the last few weeks she had slowly let go of the past. The guilt and pain had eased until they faded away like storm clouds after a summer rain.

She no longer felt weighed down by the summer heat and humidity as she stepped to the rig. The sun beat down just as mercilessly, but it didn't scorch her anymore.

Moving lightly and easily, she hoisted the cable from the hole and swung the bail bucket into place. A few minutes later she was dumping the bail bucket with its cuttings into a trough. And there it was. She blinked twice and looked again. The rainbow. Filming the water and rock was oil, pale green and reflecting the colors of the spectrum in the sunlight. Oil. She'd finally found it.

She sank down on the ground in a daze. Then slowly she began to laugh, great whoops of laughter that startled a flock of crows in the cornfield. She rolled over onto her back and grabbed fistfuls of grass in her hands, throwing them into the air. She'd finally hit oil.

She called the log survey company the day the county fair started, and they got there that morning. She had already set a four-and-a-half-inch casing to the bottom of the hole. The man working the log survey truck was jovial and rotund, with dark hair thinning on top. "Been finding a lot of oil in these parts," he said, wiping his sweaty brow with a bandanna. "First time I've seen a woman drilling though."

"I'm retiring after this one," she said. "I'm going to move away."

"Well, we'll soon get some idea if you'll have some retirement money to take with you," he said, his eyes crinkling in a smile. The bottom of the hole was plugged with a rubber and wood piece. Mr. Callum, owner of the log truck, lowered a tool into the hole and perforated the casing the depth of the shale where Cally had found the oil. He pressure-grouted the hole, pumping in acid to frack the formation—break it up to determine if it held live oil.

Cally moved to the back of the truck to watch the various instruments spew out their readings. It was strange, she thought, that she felt no excitement during all of this. The only thing on her mind at the moment was Mike Donovan.

She heard a horn honking in the driveway and went to check. It was the mailman, Pete Jordan, and he had an enormous package for her. "From St. Louis," he said, eyeing the address. "This from your young man?"

Cally nodded. "For all I know he's inside the box."

Pete shook his head. "If he is, then I probably knocked him unconscious coming down the county road. I just about hit my head on the roof what with all the ruts. Can't get the commissioners to do anything about that road." Cally leaned against the box, which looked just big enough to hold Mike, and waited until Pete had run down. "Well, see you around, Cally," he said, starting to back down the drive. "I've got to get going. That letter Mrs. Potter was expecting from her daughter came today. Best get it to her."

Cally waved, then stood back to eye the box with wary contemplation. She gave it an exploratory push with her foot, and she heard something move slightly. "You in there, Donovan?" she asked dubiously. No answer. She got a large screwdriver from the kitchen and began pulling the box apart.

Nestled on top was another box, and she opened that. Swathed in soft packing material was a teapot just like the one she'd broken. Smiling, she set it aside, then cocked a wary brow at the remainder of the package. Surely he didn't send hundreds of teacups to go with the pot.

She began pulling out white paper bags and reading the

printing on the front. "Flowers," she said in wonder. Each bag was neatly labeled. Tulips, hyacinths, daffodils—there must be hundreds and hundreds of bulbs in the box. Cally groaned. "There are enough here to plant an acre."

At the bottom was an envelope and she took out the letter.

Hi, there!
  The woman at the nursery said you'd kill me for sending this, but I assured her you were too far away to attack me at the moment. Maybe I should wear a suit of armor next time I see you. By the way, the bulbs have to be refrigerated till fall.

Refrigerated! She looked at the box, then at the house, then back to the box. "You've really done it this time, Donovan," she muttered, staring helplessly at the bulbs. But then, what could she expect from a man who'd covered a bed with roses for her?

Sighing, she picked up an armful of the white bags and started toward the house. If there was one thing Mike Donovan would never be it was dull.

She made it to the fairgrounds after talking with Mr. Callum about the readings he got. He assured her the well looked very good, but Cally still felt no jubilation.

She checked the exhibit hall for her girls' 4-H entries. There were several blue ribbons, and she knew the girls would be too excited to sleep tonight. That first blue ribbon at a county fair was something special.

She glanced at her watch and hurried toward the indoor pavilion. She passed by the snack booths, connected at the top by strings of colored light bulbs and peopled by vendors in white hats making hot dogs and pretzels and snow cones. The aroma of the food mixed with the musty smell of the sawdust laid down on the paths. Somewhere in the distance a cow bawled in her pen.

Just beyond the booths she could see the lights of the midway. The clear strains of the merry-go-round music filled the night air.

She hurried into the pavilion and found a seat in the last row of metal chairs. Laura's mother was in the front row,

Cally saw, tapping her foot impatiently while another little girl finished her demonstration on cookies. The judges sat apart from the audience, clipboards on their laps. They smiled and clapped politely when the little girl finished, and Cally watched as the next contestant set up. This little girl was making a refrigerator pie, and partway through her demonstration she forgot to put the top on the blender before she started it, and lemon filling flew into the air, one glop landing in the hair of one of the judges. The judge smiled gamely and dabbed at her hair with a napkin while the little girl hurriedly finished her presentation in an inaudible whisper.

Then it was Laura's turn. She spotted Cally in the back and smiled nervously when Cally gave her the thumbs-up sign. *Come on, Laura,* Cally implored her. *You can do it.*

Laura wasn't quite as nervous as she'd been during the club meeting, but it was obvious she wasn't confident as she began. Her voice quivered, and she kept darting hopeful glances into the audience. Poor kid, Cally thought. She's waiting for Mike to show up. Well, aren't we all? she thought irritably.

Laura's hand trembled visibly as she stirred her chocolate mixture, and again her eyes swept the audience. Cally could hardly make herself watch, and she pretended to study the program in her lap.

When Laura spoke again, her voice was noticeably stronger and more confident. "Be sure the chocolate is cool, or your brownies will be tough." Cally sat up straighter, mentally cheering Laura on as she continued the demonstration in a chatty, relaxed tone, obviously at ease. Whatever had brought about the change, Cally was grateful.

The demonstration ended as Laura pulled a pan of baked brownies from a shelf under the table and tilted them for everyone to see. "Remember," she said solemnly, "brownies should be moist and chewy, never gooey." The judges applauded, with a great deal of enthusiasm Cally noted, and she held her breath while they compared their scores. The contestants all lined up in front of the table, and the judges began giving out the ribbons. Everyone was given a ribbon for their achievement, and there were several blue. Cally smiled when Laura was awarded one of those. Then came the rankings. Third prize, a white ribbon, went to the girl who made cookies. Second, a red, went to a girl whose demonstration Cally had missed. Then came the champion ribbon, twice as large as the others and purple. The judges beamed as they handed it to Laura.

Cally leaped to her feet to applaud with the others, and Laura's face was nearly incandescent with happiness.

Someone was applauding behind Cally and she turned with a smile, saying, "She was really good, wasn't she?" Her voice broke and her hands froze when she saw Mike.

"She was wonderful," he agreed, but his eyes were on Cally, and his smile was all for her.

Laura came running toward them, and after Cally had hugged her she stood back to let the little girl proudly receive Mike's congratulations. He looked wonderful, Cally thought, her mouth going dry as she studied him.

More tan than ever, his dark good looks were set off dramatically by black slacks and a red shirt. She couldn't take her eyes off him.

When Laura ran back to her mother, Mike met Cally's gaze, and she saw the yearning in his eyes. "Want to see any more of the fair?" he asked.

She shook her head. "Let's go home."

They started out the door, hand in hand, and Mike seemed reluctant to let go of her, even when they came to Daffy parked in the field that doubled as a parking lot. "My truck's over there," he said, pointing down the row. "I'll see you at the house."

Cally broke a few personal speed records getting home, but still Mike arrived first. Her heart sank when she saw another car follow them into the driveway. It stopped and four people climbed out.

"Thought you'd be getting home right about now," John Masters called cheerfully. "We heard the good news about the log truck, and we came by to congratulate you."

Cally glanced at Mike, just shutting his door, and caught the fleeting look of surprise on his face. She hadn't told him any of this yet.

She and Mike trooped inside with John and Paula Masters and two more neighbors from down the road, the Shannons. Mrs. Shannon was a plump, florid woman in a pantsuit that encased her like a sausage, and she put a single-layer, iced chocolate cake down on the table. "Now make some coffee, Cally," she said, "and we'll celebrate this right."

Cally had the passing thought that Mrs. Shannon celebrated a lot of things with chocolate cake.

She settled everyone at the kitchen table, her eyes returning over and over to Mike, who stood leaning against the counter. "I'm sorry," she whispered as she passed him to put on the coffee.

He shrugged, but she was disturbed by the wary expression on his face.

"How does the well look?" John asked eagerly. "Good producer?"

Cally nodded. "From his readings, Mr. Callum says initial production will probably go fifteen barrels a day."

John whistled. "Sounds good."

Mr. Shannon, a tall burly man in bib overalls, leaned back in his chair. "Well, Cally, I guess you'll be adding to your herd now. Why, you'll be able to afford that herd of Herefords Dan was always talking about."

She gave him a stiff smile and nodded, her eyes darting to Mike again. His expression had grown more closed, and now he looked at the floor.

"You can get a new combine," Paula said in wonder. She massaged her gnarled fingers in her lap. "Just think of that. And a new truck. You know, you really need a new truck, Cally. You should buy that first."

They all began talking at once, recommending trucks and farm machinery and increased cattle production. From the corner of her eye, Cally saw Mike move quietly toward the stairs, and she watched him helplessly. He didn't turn back to look at her, and she knotted her hands.

The Shannons and Masterses were all keyed up about the oil well, and John began making plans to drill more holes on his land. "When do you reckon you could start drilling again, Mike?" he said, turning in his chair. He looked back at Cally, and she said, "He went upstairs to wash up. He just got in."

"And I bet he's tired," John said apologetically. "Listen, we just wanted to congratulate you on this. It's just wonderful."

Mr. Shannon launched into another excited discussion of hog production, and it was another half hour before they all stood to leave. Cally thanked them for coming, the minutes dragging as they shuffled slowly toward the door. She forced herself to stand at the door, smiling and waving, until they backed down the drive. When she got to the stairs, she took them two at a time. But she stopped at the top in disappointment when she saw the closed door. He'd already gone to bed. Well, she'd waited this long. She could wait until morning to tell him.

The smell of coffee woke her, and she glanced at the clock. It was barely six. What was he doing awake so early? He must be tired.

She pulled on a blouse and pair of jeans, fastening them as she hurried downstairs. He was sitting at the kitchen table, a cup of coffee in front of him, and the cold expression on his face brought her up short. Her smile died on her lips.

He glanced at his watch and stood up. "I thought I'd get an early start back."

"Back?" she repeated dumbly. "You just got here. I haven't even had a hello kiss, and you're leaving." She was fast growing angry.

"Look, it was a mistake for me to come," he said. "I've got things to do back home."

"Wouldn't you like a little breakfast before you go?" she asked with gritted teeth. "Or don't you have time?"

"Just something light," he said, shrugging.

"Light would be fine," she said, her voice rising. "You can have dry toast or cereal without milk."

"What did you do, run out of food again?" he demanded, his voice finally showing some emotion.

"I have no food because my refrigerator is filled to the gills with flower bulbs," she said, a high-pitched squeak emphasizing her annoyance, "and they'll be there until the fall."

"Oh." At least he looked somewhat sheepish.

"Yes, oh. So I suggest we go to the diner and have a decent breakfast, and then we can talk."

Her words were clipped and brooked no argument. She marched out the kitchen door, and Mike followed her. She could tell from his quick stride that he was not happy. Cally's truck was behind his, and she climbed in the driver's side without another thought.

"I hope you aren't planning to strand us on Zimmer's Bridge again," he said caustically as he opened the door.

"Get in," Cally said, sniffing. "Harley's brother fixed it. I haven't had any trouble."

He looked skeptical, but he got in without another word. In fact, barely a word passed between them all the way to the diner. Well, almost all the way. They were approximately fifty feet from the parking lot when Daffy sputtered with wracking coughs and died right in the middle of the road. Mike looked at Cally triumphantly. "Ah ha!"

"Don't be so happy about it," she snapped. "It almost got us there."

He gave her a patient smile over bared teeth that made her shrink against the door. "May I remind you that someone will now have to push this monstrosity off the road. Any volunteers?"

"My, my, but we're surly before breakfast," she retorted.

His snarl when he slammed the door reminded her of the tiger cage at the St. Louis zoo just before feeding time.

He pushed the truck into the parking lot and stood watching grimly while she alighted nonchalantly, as if they'd arrived under Daffy's own power. His hand was a trifle tighter than comfortable on her arm as they entered the diner. Gordon was in the process of smashing a fly on the counter with a rolled-up newspaper, and he nodded a tacit greeting.

Only two booths were occupied, one with three farmers and the other with a middle-aged couple who looked as though they were on vacation. Cally suspected they belonged to the car with the out-of-state license plate.

Cally led Mike to the back booth where they had sat the last time and settled herself with dignity.

"Reba's late," Gordon grumbled, setting two spotty glasses of water in front of them and handing them each a grease-stained menu. He wiped a few crumbs off the table with the end of his apron.

"I'll take the hotcake special," Cally said without opening the menu.

"Two eggs over easy, toast, and coffee," Mike said tersely.

Gordon gathered the menus and moved away without comment, and Cally busied herself drawing circles with her water glass.

"It's comforting to know you can now afford to buy yourself a new truck with all your recent wealth," Mike said coolly. "Or do you actually prefer undependable heaps?"

"I must," she retorted. "I hooked up with you."

She saw his teeth clench as he glowered at her over the table.

"I'm glad about the oil well, Cally," he ground out. "I really am."

"You have a funny way of showing it," she said dryly. "I haven't seen that kind of enthusiasm since the hogs ate fermented apples."

"I certainly didn't expect to be informed of your success by a welcome party on your doorstep," he said, his voice growing louder. "When did you plan to tell me? After you made your first million?"

"If you will recall," she said in acid tones, "you showed up last night with absolutely no warning, unless you count those million bulbs you sent. I didn't have a chance to tell you. I only struck oil yesterday. What did you expect? A billboard at the city limits?" The three farmers had turned to watch them, one of them still eating as he rested his plate on the back of the seat.

"It doesn't matter now anyway," Mike said, his tone just a hair below a shout. "You're the future cattle baron of Prairie Junction. In a year or two, you'll be rolling in cow chips." His sardonic smile looked exactly like a sneer to her.

"What are cow chips?" the woman tourist asked her husband, pushing up her tinted glasses and adjusting her skirt.

"Shhh," he hushed her quickly. "I want to find out why he sent her a million light bulbs."

"For your information, Mike Donovan," Cally said, rising to her feet and resting her hands on the table, "I was planning on moving to St. Louis with you. But I think I'd prefer living with the hogs."

"Well, that's just fine," Mike retorted, standing up to face her angrily across the table, "because I sold the St. Louis apartment."

"That's just dandy," she said with the air of someone about to top him. "Because I just sold the farm."

Comprehension dawned, and they stared at each other, thunderstruck. "You sold the farm?" Mike asked in disbelief. "But all that talk last night about new farm equipment and more cattle . . ."

Cally shrugged helplessly. "I hadn't told anyone, because I wanted you to know first. Donna had a buyer, and I called her yesterday and told her to go ahead and sell. It didn't bring much. I kept the oil rights, of course."

"You sold the farm," he repeated, a lopsided smile lighting his face.

"And what was the idea of sending all those bulbs?" she demanded. "And then selling your apartment?"

He cleared his throat. "I already dug the foundation for our new house on the property in southern Missouri where we camped. I thought you'd want to plant the bulbs there. I guess I should have asked you first." He sounded somewhat chagrined.

"It'll take me months to get those bulbs planted," she groaned. A bewildered smile crossed her face. "Donovan, where are we going to live? We both sold our homes."

"That's what I'd like to know," the woman said from her booth, and her husband shushed her again.

Mike's enthusiasm returned. "We can camp out this summer and by fall I'll have the outside shell finished. We can live in it this winter while we complete the inside."

"When are you going to have time to build a house?" she demanded, putting her hands on her hips. "If you expect me to hammer nails and saw wood and pour concrete you've got another think coming. Nosiree." She shook her head vehemently. "I'm not building that house while you're off drilling somewhere."

"Cally." He reached across the table and took her hand. "I won't be off drilling anywhere. I'm going to stay right there at home with you. I can run the business from there. It's something I should have done a long time ago, anyway.

The business is turning a handsome profit now. It's about time I settled down and really ran it." He grinned at her ruefully. "The only problem is I think our phone's going to be in a tree until we get the house finished."

"Donovan," she said solemnly. "You're stark raving mad." She leaned across the table toward him, and he cupped her chin.

"Does that mean you'll marry me?" he asked.

She nodded. "Was there ever any doubt?"

"Never," he answered, his mouth closing on hers. Kissing him across a table in Gordon's Grill wasn't the best, but it was better than not kissing him at all. Her eyes flew open when she heard cheers and applause, and she looked into Mike's amused gaze just inches from her. "Just the kibitzers," he murmured, kissing her again.

"Tell you what," she whispered against his lips. "After breakfast, let's see if we can't get my truck to break down in a more private place. Like, say Zimmer's Bridge."

"We could be marooned there all day," he said with a lazy grin. "You know how temperamental that truck is."

"Here's your breakfast," Gordon said with his usual lack of enthusiasm, setting the plates on the table and wiping his fingers on his apron, which only served to transfer more grease to his hands.

Mike disengaged himself from Cally, thanked Gordon and walked around the table to sit beside her. "You know," he said, putting his arm around her, "I'll have to bring you back here every anniversary. We can check on the oil wells."

Cally looked down at her plate of burned hotcakes, grease from the griddle coagulating on the side. "Your men do that. Why don't you just send me flowers?"

"Flowers," he said, brightening. "Now there's a novel idea."

"Oh, no," Cally groaned. "A house with wall-to-wall flowers."

"This is better than Disneyland was, Harold," the woman said enthusiastically.

"I hope you still want lots of kids," Mike said. "I want the first to be a girl, so she can cook brownies with you."

"That's bake brownies, Donovan. I can see right now

what kind of life we're going to have."

"Blissfully happy," he murmured, nuzzling her neck with his mouth.

"Ummm," she agreed, her power of speech waning as his fingers trailed through her hair. "Blissfully."

WONDERFUL ROMANCE NEWS!

Do you know about the exciting SECOND CHANCE AT LOVE/TO HAVE AND TO HOLD newsletter? Are you on our *free* mailing list? If reading all about your favorite authors, getting sneak previews of their latest releases, and being filled in on all the latest happenings and events in the romance world sound good to you, then you'll love our SECOND CHANCE AT LOVE and TO HAVE AND TO HOLD Romance News.

If you'd like to be added to our mailing list, just fill out the coupon below and send it in…and we'll send you your *free* newsletter every three months—hot off the press.

☐ *Yes, I would like to receive your free SECOND CHANCE AT LOVE/TO HAVE AND TO HOLD newsletter.*

Name _____

Address _____

City _____ **State/Zip** _____

Please return this coupon to:

Berkley Publishing
200 Madison Avenue, New York, New York 10016
Att: Rebecca Kaufman

HERE'S WHAT READERS ARE SAYING ABOUT

Second Chance at Love

"I think your books are great. I love to read them, as does my family."
— *P. C., Milford, MA**

"Your books are some of the best romances I've read."
— *M. B., Zeeland, MI**

"SECOND CHANCE AT LOVE is my favorite line of romance novels."
— *L. B., Springfield, VA**

"I think SECOND CHANCE AT LOVE books are terrific. I married my 'Second Chance' over 15 years ago. I truly believe love is lovelier the second time around!"
— *P. P., Houston, TX**

"I enjoy your books tremendously."
— *I. S., Bayonne, NJ**

"I love your books and read them all the time. Keep them coming—they're just great."
— *G. L., Brookfield, CT**

"SECOND CHANCE AT LOVE books are definitely the best!"
— *D. P., Wabash, IN**

*Name and address available upon request